# OPERATION GLENN MILLER

# OPERATION GLENN MILLER

## Leo Kessler

| | |
|---|---|
| TALNET | |
| GW2746034 | |
| Cypher | 18.02.05 |
| | £18.99 |
| | |

**Severn House Large Print**
London & New York

This first large print edition published in Great Britain 2002 by
SEVERN HOUSE LARGE PRINT BOOKS LTD of
9-15, High Street, Sutton, Surrey, SM1 1DF.
First world regular print edition published 2001 by
Severn House Publishers, London and New York.
This first large print edition published in the USA 2003 by
SEVERN HOUSE PUBLISHERS INC., of
595 Madison Avenue, New York, NY 10022

British Library Cataloguing in Publication Data

Kessler, Leo, 1926 -
    Operation Glenn Miller - Large print ed. - (S.S. Wotan series)
    1.  Miller, Glenn, 1904 – 1944 - Fiction
    2.  World War, 1939 – 1945 - Campaigns - Fiction
    3.  War stories
    4.  Large type books
    I.  Title
    823.9'14 [F]

ISBN 0-7278-7177-3

Printed and bound in Great Britain by
MPG Books Ltd, Bodmin, Cornwall.

'Next to letters from home, the Glenn Miller Army Air Force Band was the greatest morale builder we had'

*General Jimmy Doolittle,*
*Commander General of the*
*US 8th Air Force in Britain*


'If Intelligence wasn't at fault, who then was?'

*Sir Kenneth Strong,*
*General Eisenhower's*
*Chief of Intelligence*


'Glenn Miller von der SS ermordet?'

*Welt am Sonntag 1998*

# Author's Note

At seven o'clock on the evening of Sunday 24 December 1944, Supreme Allied Headquarters in Paris made the startling announcement. One minute later, BBC London repeated the statement. It read:

Major Alton Glenn Miller, Director of the famous United States Army Air Force Band which has been playing in Paris, is reported missing while on a flight from England to Paris. The plane in which he was a passenger left England on December 15 and no trace of it has been found since its take-off. Major Miller, one of the outstanding orchestra leaders in the United States, lived in Tenafly, New Jersey, where his wife presently resides. No members of Major Miller's Band were with him on the missing plane.

The news that Glenn Miller, movie star and perhaps the Free World's most popular musical entertainer that year, was missing struck home like a bombshell. What had happened?

A little later that snowy Christmas Eve, just before the Miller swing band was going to broadcast to the United States from the Paris Olympia Theatre, further details of what had supposedly happened were released by the US military authorities on the Continent. Apparently on Friday 15 December, Glenn Miller had set off in a small Norseman passenger aircraft from a temporary wartime landing strip at Twinwood Farm, piloted by a young US second lieutenant of vaguely British origin. Its destination had been Orly, outside Paris. Miller was bound for Shaef HQ to plan a band concert for his Air Force Band which was to remain in the UK until details had been finalised. The Norseman had not reached its destination. According to the official statements and press handouts at the time, it was most likely that the bad weather – fog and rain – had forced the plane off course. It was probable that the Norseman had come down in the Channel. At all events no trace had been found since the first search for it and Major Miller.

And there the matter ended. After all, although Miller was such a famous entertainer, Eisenhower was in the midst of fighting the biggest battle of his career in the snowbound Ardennes, one that would, in the end, involve well over two million soldiers: the Battle of the Bulge. All the same, even while directing what some historians have called 'America's Gettysburg of the twentieth century', Eisenhower took a direct interest in Miller's fate. But as far as can be found out *now*, it is clear that 'Ike' preferred to have the details of Miller's disappearance hushed up.

It was seven days after the Norseman vanished that Eisenhower wrote to General Davis of his staff that he ought to send a casualty report to the War Department in Washington, reporting Miller as 'missing'. However, the General was not to do so till Christmas Eve two days later. All the same, with two days to go, Eisenhower did not order a complete search of the area of the Channel where it was thought the Norseman could have gone down. It was the same with the PR announcement. Eisenhower requested the return of the original statement and release. But the clincher and most suspicious circumstance of all, which Eisenhower would have been able to discover by means of a simple telephone call, was the 'RAF Daily History', Form 540, kept for Twinwood Farm and dated Friday December 15 1944. It reads: 'NO FLYING TODAY. AIRFIELD CLOSED.'

So if Major Glenn Miller and his young pilot did not take off in the Norseman from

Twinwood Farm Airfield that overcast, grey Friday, one week before the last Christmas of World War Two, what did happen to them? What was the fate of an entertainer, whose music is still played almost daily to this very day, nearly sixty years after he officially disappeared?

Since that December announcement, authorised by no less a person than Eisenhower, the future president of the United States, there have been literally scores of researchers – and crackpots – who have attempted to discover what happened to Glenn Miller. There have been at least a dozen books on the subject. Nearly every year the newspapers publish 'a startling new theory'. Even as the author writes one of the world's greatest news channels is preparing a documentary which will, naturally, explain all.

And what theories they have all come up with over the years! Miller's Norseman was hit by the bombs from an RAF squadron of Bomber Command. On that Friday they had jettisoned their bombs over the Channel after an abortive raid on the Reich. Unfortunately they hadn't spotted Miller's light plane flying below them ... Miller was involved in the Parisian black market. He'd gotten in with the mob. They had killed him and deposited his murdered body outside the Sphinx Club in the French capital's red light district. Naturally that had had to be hushed up ... He was caught up in an accident which caused him to be terribly disfigured and mentally confused. He was shipped home secretly under another identity and died in a stateside mental hospital ... Miller had been caught up in a sinister plot engineered by the American OSS, the forerunner of the CIA, and had paid the price for his involvement. The consequence? His file had been doctored and blocked by the National Security Agency ever since. And so on and so on.

So what did happen to Major Glenn Miller, whose recordings of 'In the Mood' and 'Little Brown Jug' epitomise World War Two for millions of people, old and young, all over the world? What transpired after Miller was last seen, according to reliable reports, at two thirty on the afternoon of Tuesday December 14 1944 outside the Milroy Club in London's Mayfair? This is a modest and perhaps final attempt to tell the truth.

*L. Kessler, Luxembourg City, December 2000*

# Book One
# The Plot

*Wer mit dem Teufel isst,*
*braucht einen langen Löffel.'*
German Proverb

# Berlin Bloodbath

# July 20 1944

# One

'Would you stick it in to me, Kuno,' Countess von Sommerfeld asked in that cool Prussian manner of hers, 'when we have finished our tea? It's been so long, I really do feel the need for a really good thrust.' To emphasise her words she rubbed her black-silk-clad legs against Kuno von Dodenburg's thigh and smiled carefully but winningly.

Obersturmbannführer von Dodenburg, erstwhile commander of SS Assault Regiment Wotan, looked at Klara von Sommerfeld in some wonder. He remembered her from before the war on their vast estates in East Prussia, when she was a sunburned, barefoot schoolkid at the local *Volksschule*. How prudish she had been then! Why, she had even refused to 'play doctor', when all the other infant countesses and baronnesses had been only too eager to take off their knickers and play patients to the little boys' doctors. Now, elegant in her black widow's weeds, with her husband hardly beneath the earth in some godforsaken Polish field of

17

battle, and she was offering to go upstairs with him in her suite at Berlin's Hotel Adlon for what she called so crudely 'a really good thrust'.

'Well,' she demanded and took a sip of the ersatz tea from the Adlon's Meissen, 'have you lost your taste for German women over these last years?' Over the rim of her cup, she stared at him with her ice-cold, blue eyes and told herself that despite his haggard, battle-worn face, Kuno was as harshly handsome as he had ever been; indeed more so. In bed she imagined he would be as virile and as sharp as a cut-throat razor. She shivered slightly at the thought and her excellent breasts trembled under the sheer black silk of her frock. Hans-Albert, her late and unlamented husband, had simply torn the clothes off her and thrust it in her, back or front, without a moment's thought whether she was satisfied or not. Kuno von Dodenburg would be different. Arrogant as he was, she guessed he'd know all the tricks.

The Adlon was beginning to fill up now. It didn't matter that the Reich was on its last legs, with the enemy fighting almost on Germany's borders to east and west; the swanky Berlin hotel-restaurant always filled up at tea time. Naturally, anybody who was somebody in the capital wanted to be seen at the Adlon.

Von Dodenburg sniffed. He didn't like

what he saw. The fat generals with the red stripe of the general staff down the side of their elegant uniforms, escorting their girl mistresses in French fashions; self-important businessmen – fat, greasy – hurrying to yet another deal; 'golden pheasants'; fat-bellied Party bosses in their brown uniforms, covered in gold braid, again with teenage mistresses, bullying the waiters with the power invested in them by the mis-named German Workers' Party. And at the front the 'stubble-hoppers' were dying like flies.

'Klara,' he began, 'you must realise why I'm here. *Not* for pleasure. Wotan is crying out for reinforcements. We're bleeding to death in the west. The Regiment needs bodies—' He stopped short and gave a little gasp. With her free hand she had reached under the table and was fumbling with his flies. *'Klara!'*

She smiled in that hard way of hers, as if it took an effort to do so. 'Forget the war, Kuno,' she said and ran her tongue round her thin pink lips provocatively. 'What does it matter? It's all too late.' She shrugged and her little, pointed breasts beneath the sheer black silk trembled once more. 'You're going to die. I am. As they say, the peace is going to be terrible, let's enjoy the war.' Her cunning fingers penetrated inside his open flies and fondled his penis. Despite the place and his mood, he felt himself hardening. She noted the stiffening, too, and said softly, 'Now Kuno, isn't that better than worrying about the silly front? If you need bodies, I am perfectly willing to sacrifice mine.' She pressed his penis even harder.

'Klara,' he began again, but once more she cut him short. 'I've got a bottle of bubbly upstairs. I knew you wouldn't object. Had the room waiter put it on ice just before you came. Should be nice and chilled. French, of course, none of your German *Sekt* rubbish.' She stroked his stiff penis more gently now, her sense of urgency vanished, as if she knew she had convinced him; he was hers. She'd get what she wanted now. 'Give me an hour till cocktails and then you can go back to your stupid war.' She sighed and took away her hand.

Hastily, feeling that he had gone red because everyone in the crowded Adlon's gilt and white tearoom must have been well aware of what this pretty war widow in her elegant black frock and hat (complete with regulation veil) was doing to him under the table, von Dodenburg did up his flies.

Her grin increased at his discomfiture. She leaned forward and whispered huskily, eyes gleaming in a very naughty fashion. 'Don't tuck that delightful love stick away too much ... I wouldn't want it to get too cosy. If you follow me?' She raised her voice and drained the rest of her milkless tea; for even the Adlon sometimes ran out of rationed foodstuffs. 'Now, my dear Kuno, do you think you could *limp* upstairs with me and forget that damned war of yours?'

But that wasn't to be. In the same instant that she replaced the delicate Meissen porcelain cup on its saucer, the loud-speakers with which even the Adlon was equipped by law burst into noisy metallic life: '*Achtung ... achtung,*' the harsh voice commanded, '*Hier spricht der Reichsführer für Propaganda: und Volksaufklarung Herr Doktor Goebbels.*'

As one the guests in that crowded elegant room fell silent. Even the generals of the General Staff and the fat-bellied, swaggering Party bosses wouldn't have continued to speak over the 'Poison Dwarf', as they called the undersized, club-footed Minister behind his back. 'Great crap on the Christmas shitting tree,' Klara von Sommerfeld cursed and then went silent too.

'Folk Comrades,' Goebbels' incisive Rhenish voice came over the speakers, distorted by them a little, but still as penetrating and effective as ever, 'at twelve forty hours this morning a dastardly attack was made on the life of our beloved Führer, Adolf Hitler.'

There was a gasp from that arrogant, self-satisfied crowd as if someone had just slid a sharp blade into their collective gut. Even

21

Klara turned pale. Somewhere a waiter dropped his tray with a noisy clatter. No one looked round. The announcement was too shocking for trivia like that.

'But as always,' Goebbels went on (like the trained orator and rabblerouser that he was, he always knew to the fraction of a second when to end a pause for the maximum effect) 'divine providence has protected our beloved Führer from the cowardly treacherous attack. Adolf Hitler is slightly shaken. *But he lives!*' His voice rose and his listeners responded immediately, just as the unseen speaker had anticipated they would. There was a burst of fervent clapping. Here and there men cried, *'Thank God!'* A fat woman, who bore the 'Mother Cross' in silver and blue enamel around her thick neck, heavy with goitre, started to sob. Even Kuno von Dodenburg, who had long finished with the Party and its corrupt bosses, felt a sudden tightening of his lean gut.

'Perfidious creatures most probably working for our enemies, those Jewish Anglo-American plutocrats led by that old sot Churchill and the Jewish cripple Roosevelt, planted a bomb at the Führer's HQ just behind the fighting front.'

Kuno could have smiled at that 'just behind the front'. In fact, the Führer HQ at Rastenburg was hundreds of kilometres away from the fighting. But he didn't; he

22

was too shocked by this totally unexpected development.

'Several of the Führer's closest comrades have been seriously injured by the bomb. But retribution is taking place at this very moment, Folk Comrades. Indeed, four of the leading traitors have already been shot. There will be more. We have to root out this evil without further delay. Folk Comrades, I wish you now to join me in sending our beloved Leader our warmest best wishes, in assuring him that he will have our undying loyalty and that there is not one of us, man, woman and child, who wouldn't lay down his life for him without the slightest hesitation. *Volksgenossen ... Heil Hitler ... Sieg heil!*'

As a military band broke into the national anthem on the radio, all bass drum and high brass, the whole room rose to its feet, stretched out their right arms and bellowed back at the loudspeakers. *'Heil Hitler ... Sieg heil.'*

Goebbels' voice disappeared with the band. As the brassy blare of that bombastic anthem died away, another and harsher voice took over. With military precision the unknown speaker rasped, 'There will be a curfew tonight from 2200 hours. All civilian and military personnel will clear the streets except for those with special permission ... Listening to foreign radio stations will be punished by death...' On and on the

23

commands went, all relating to the grave crisis into which the Reich had been plunged by the attempt on the Führer's life. Just by chance a dazed and confused Kuno von Dodenburg caught the order, 'All Waffen SS officers above the rank of captain will report immediately to the Berlin office of Jagdkommando Skorzeny without delay.'

Klara looked up at von Dodenburg. Instinctively, she pressed his hard dry hand. 'Don't go,' she said in a low voice. 'You know Skorzeny.'

Kuno von Dodenburg did know the hulking Viennese giant with his scarface which looked like the work of a crazy butcher. He was the head of the SS's own special forces, a born killer and adventurer, who would stop at nothing. He was a highly dangerous man.

'He'll get you killed,' Klara said pleadingly, hiding her mouth with her hand, as if Skorzeny's commandos might be watching her at this very moment. 'Nobody knows you're here. How could they? You're straight from the front. Stay with me ... we can put up here. I'll do anything you like ... in bed and out.' She leaned forward and whispered obscenities into his right ear. 'Any one of those you can do to me.' There was a note of crazy pleading in her voice now. 'Fuck me backwards, forwards, upside down, if you wish. *Anything* ... I don't care what...' Her pleading faded away to nothing. It was no use, for Kuno had already released his hand from her grip, gently but firmly.

She stood there, shoulders suddenly drooped in defeat. She knew she would never see him again. Kuno von Dodenburg would never 'stick it into her' now.

'*Achtung ... achtung*,' the loudspeakers were still blaring, as he walked out of the doors of the Adlon in a daze, '*alle Offiziere der Waffen SS werden sich sofort melden.*' Automatically Kuno returned the salute of the ancient porter in his braided uniform that made him look like a field marshal down on his luck. Above, the July sky was changing. Rapidly, the hot red ball of the sun was disappearing behind a black cloud. There was going to be a storm.

It was 20 July 1944. The world had changed this day. For Germany there was no going back now. Automatically, Obersturmbannführer von Dodenburg squared his shoulders and lengthened his stride, as proud as he had been back in the great days when he had goose-stepped down these same Berlin streets at the head of his bold, blond young giants. But there was no going back now for Kuno von Dodenburg, either.

Now it was, in the lethal motto of SS Assault Regiment Wotan, *march or croak*.

# Two

Berlin's Le Charité hospital was going wild.

Flares hissed into the night. Time and time again they exploded in a burst of blood-red flame. Everywhere the lights were switched on despite the blackout. Wounded soldiers in their blue and white striped pjyamas hung out of the windows shouting crazily, waving looted bottles of surgical spirit and crying, 'The war's over!' Even the humble, half-starved Russian POW orderlies joined in with their, *'Voina kaputt!'*

Down in the courtyard, Senior Sister Edeltraut, sixty if she was a day, was running wildly for the gate, skirt high about her spindly shanks, chased by a double amputee in a wheelchair, crying, 'He'll rape me ... help ... he'll rape me!' while the drunken sentries urged the wounded soldier on, yelling above the confused racket, 'Get to it, Franz ... We'll help yer on the old cow ... *Ride 'em, cowboy!*'

Naturally, Sergeant Schulze and his old running mate Matz were drunk, but not *that* drunk. The two 'old hares' of SS Assault

Regiment Wotan had an eye to the main chance. Crazy situations like this were just made for the two rogues. Now they and their disparate band were prepared for what Matz, who had his wooden leg over his shoulder and was drinking looted beer out of a chamber pot, called 'the big snatch': a phrase which had Schulze giggling uncontrollably for a while before he raised his right thigh thoughtfully.

Now he farted in that not unmusical fashion of his which was celebrated throughout the SS NCO Corps and which had several of his disparate band of robbers gasping as if in the final throes of an asthma attack, and announced, 'Comrades, old Adolf's snuffed it, the war's over, and now it's the time of yer old hairy-arsed stubble-hopper, ain't it?'

There was a murmur of agreement from the other wounded soldiers, save from One Ball, who grabbed for the metal box which protected his injured testicles and moaned, 'Schulzi, keep it down to a frigging low roar, willya? That noise shakes me old ball something awful.' He winced, as if in acute pain.

As always Sergeant Schulze showed no tolerance of weakness in others. He threw One Ball a look of contempt. 'Hold yer frigging water ... and get a grip o' yourself.' He laughed. 'Though by the look of that poxy love tool o' yourn, you won't be getting a grip o' yourself for a long time, if ever!' He made an explicit obscene gesture with a fist that looked like a small steam shovel.

The others joined in and Nose – he'd had his nose shot by a Russian explosive bullet outside Warsaw – snorted, blowing snot and blood out of the twin holes which now adorned the centre of his ugly mug, 'Perhaps they'll be able to give him an artificial nut. Sew it on, like.'

'I'll sew something else on you, if you don't frigging well shut up,' Schulze rapped. 'Now get this.'

They strained. One didn't disobey Sergeant Schulze's orders lightly, if one didn't want to lose a set of good teeth. In the yard the younger nurses, drunk beyond all reason, were performing a striptease to the delight of the wounded, while a bunch of the lighter cases accompanied their nubile gyrations with spoons and paper and combs. Under any other circumstances, Sergeant Schulze would have dropped everything and watched. It wasn't every day that the former cream of the Association of German Maidens revealed their fleshy charms to common soldiers. But not now. He admonished his listeners with, 'Get yer frigging glassy orbs off'n them tits and listen to me.'

They listened.

'Now we're sitting on a gold mine here,

28

comrades. Yer all know that the Reichsmark is only good enough to wipe yer arse on. That surgical spirit the other silly shits have looted softens yer frigging brain.' He paused and dramatically raised his forefinger, which looked like a hairy pork sausage, his broad face glowing in triumph in the ruddy light of the flares. 'So what is this gold mine?' Schulze answered his own question, *'Penicillin*!' He beamed at the others like a magician who had just successfully pulled a white rabbit out of his top hat.

Slowly, very slowly, Matz lowered the chamber pot filled with good Munich beer. 'And what,' he said icily, 'is this pen ... pencillin stuff, may I ask, Senior Sergeant Schulze?'

Schulze was in no way offended by the cheeky question from a lowly acting corporal. He answered in an urbane fashion for him – in other words, he didn't bellow at the top of his voice as if he were dealing with a bunch of deaf, congenital idiots, 'Only the best cure for pox known to man. A couple o' shots of that stuff in yer arse and they tell me yer stop pissing in ten different directions straightaway. It's the new magic bullet, Matzi, old house.'

Matz whistled softly, suitably impressed. 'Holy strawsack,' he exclaimed, 'that really is something. All them whores and pavement pounders'd pay a frigging fortune for

29

something like that. They'd never go out of business!'

'*Exactment*, as they say in Chink,' Schulze agreed, 'and there's thousands more who'd buy it. Now, pin back yer lugholes. Back in France our lot captured a wagonload of this penicillin stuff and brought it here to the Charité for trials. Naturally, the sawbones started stealing it themsens. Half of them doctors is poxed up to the eyeballs as it is,' he added scornfully, 'but there's still plenty of the stuff left ... and comrades, we're gonna get it. Now that the war's over, we might as well start providing oursens with a war pension ... especially you lot of frigging cripples.'

'Who you calling cripples?' Matz objected, busy now strapping on his wooden leg in readiness for the action to come.

Schulze ignored the comment. 'All right,' he commanded, 'follow old Sarge. He knows where the stuff is hid. *Los!*' Hardly pausing to squeeze the large breasts of one of the drunken nurses who had staggered, completely naked, into the little group of wounded SS men, Schulze led them inside.

With one swift kick of his big boot, he smashed down the door with its warning, 'OUT OF BOUNDS TO ALL UNAUTHOR- IZED PERSONNEL. Signed the Hospital Commandant'. It splintered as if it were made of matchwood. The little group

30

stopped. In front of them there was case upon case of the new wonder drug, as Schulze had called it, each stencilled with the legend, 'US Army Medical Corps. Store in a Cool Place.'

None of them could read English, but they recognised the US Army stencil easily enough. One Ball whistled softly and said, 'They must have a lot o' siff and pox, the Amis.'

Schulze roared with delight at the sight and exclaimed, 'The Yanks'd rather fuck than fight. Them Ami Yids is a clever lot, not like us shitting stupid Germans. No matter, comrades, let's get it. Lovely grub!' He rubbed his big paws in anticipation of the fun and high jinks which the drug would buy in the days to come and then grabbed for the nearest case. He never made it.

Behind him a familiar voice said in that cool if somewhat arrogant tone with which Sergeant Schulze and the rest had been long familiar, 'Sergeant Schulze, Matz and the rest of you rogues, get your thieving paws off those cases.'

They turned and as one clicked, the best they could, to attention.

'It's the old man—' Matz gasped and stopped short as Obersturmbannführer von Dodenburg, looking haggard but yet very alert, beat him to it with a curt smile and the words, 'Yes, the old man, Corporal Matz.'

He looked around at their surprised faces. 'In the devil's name, what a bunch o' crooks you are. Can't turn my back on you for a moment. Going and getting yourselves shot up like this. You're a disgrace to the Armed SS and the NCO corps.' His haggard, pinched face relaxed for a moment. 'Good to see you. Makes me feel at home again, leading you lot of shirkers and sharp dealers.' His smile vanished almost as quickly as it had appeared. 'Now then, lads, I've got a job for you...'

Two hours earlier, after the orderly had woken him from a drugged sleep filled with vision of a naked, wicked Klara von Sommerfeld offering him her dead husband's head on a silver platter like some latter-day Salome – along with various parts of her anatomy at the same time – he had been hurried into the presence of the head of the Waffen SS's Jagdkommando.

Skorzeny looked bigger even than in his pictures in the papers and the newsreels the time he had rescued the Italian dictator Mussolini from his mountain-top prison back in 1943. The duelling scars from student days in his native Vienna seemed worse too. Half his face appeared to have been severed and then crudely stitched together once again. He looked up but didn't rise, although Kuno von Dodenburg outranked him. But then, von Dodenburg told himself somewhat cynically, the big Austrian show-off was used to dealing solely with bigshots these days. It was said he was the Führer's own special favourite. 'Skorzeny,' he said without the customary military formality. 'You wanted me.'

Skorzeny, who had been a junior officer under von Dodenburg's command back in Russia in '41, recognised him naturally and turned on the old Viennese charm, as frothy, sugary and as meaningless as that whipped cream with which the Austrians had once smothered the top of their coffees. 'How good of you to come, von Dodenburg ... and may I say what a pleasure it is to see you again, although we meet under the worst possible circumstances.' Finally he remembered to stretch out his hand in welcome. Von Dodenburg ignored it. Instead he said in that clipped accent that had frozen many a fresh-faced young lieutenant to the ground with fear, 'Where's the shitting fire?'

Skorzeny ignored the insult. He continued to smile and said, 'The Bendlerstrasse.' He meant the headquarters of the Greater German General Staff. 'Those damned monocle Fritzes, as the Führer calls them, have gone and betrayed him. They're behind this perfidious assassination attempt.'

'I see,' von Dodenburg said without any apparent surprise, though his brain was racing. He and his friends all belonged to those 'monocle Fritzes', the aristocratic Prussian military caste. 'And my role?'

'You are to take whatever men from your old command you can find here in Berlin hospitals, the old "Bodyguard" barracks at Lichtefelde, the Reserve Battalion,' Skorzeny shrugged his big brutal shoulders, 'anywhere...'

'And march them to the Bendlerstrasse.' Von Dodenburg beat Skorzeny to it.

'Exactly.'

'And do what, Skorzeny?'

'Supervise the shootings.'

This time von Dodenburg was really taken off guard. 'Of whom?' he managed to gasp.

'Those red-striped bastards of generals who have just attempted to assassinate the Führer.'

'The Greater General Staff!'

'Not all of them, von Dodenburg. Though I don't doubt that the whole corrupt bunch of them is involved one way or the other. But we need some of them for the future. Unfortunately. I'll give you the list of those still to be shot.'

'But on whose authority?' von Dodenburg protested, finding his voice at last, for he was shocked beyond measure. In the middle of a life-or-death war you didn't shoot your most experienced generals and staff officers.

Skorzeny shrugged carelessly. 'Who cares? They're traitors, aren't they?'

Now, as von Dodenburg faced his motley bunch of Wotan troopers, veterans the lot and all hard as nails, he thought of Skorzeny's final words. They didn't please him. They smacked of total, one hundred per cent cynicism. Had the Third Reich that had promised a 'New Order' which would cleanse an old and decadent Europe come to this?

Sergeant Schulze, normally not the most sensitive of men, seemed to be able to read his young CO's troubled mind, for he said, 'Sir?'

'Yes, Schulze?'

'I think we'd better be off, sir ... it's getting late.'

'Yes, Schulze,' von Dodenburg answered, hardly recognising his own voice, which appeared to be coming from a very long way off, 'you're right ... it *is* getting late.' But how late, the big loyal NCO with the broad boozer's face and broken nose could not even imagine...

# Three

'Please don't...' The old officer's plea for help ended in a thick gurgle as the SS medical orderly thrust back his head brutally with a threatening, 'Hold yer head still, you bald-headed bastard!'

Von Dodenburg winced.

Outside in the courtyard of the Bendlerstrasse War Ministry they were shooting staff officers once more. They'd just cleared away the last lot, throwing dead bodies into the backs of trucks like logs of wood. Now a platoon of SS officers were firing their machine pistols into the supposed traitors, each victim ringed by the ice-blue light of truck headlights. Von Dodenburg told himself that what was happening here this night was not just murder, it was the massacre of the Prussian officer caste: the same class to which he himself belonged, save that he was on the winning side this time, the SS.

'Give me the shitting thread, for God's sake,' the sweating SS doctor in his short sleeves cried angrily. 'How the devil do you expect me to save the treacherous bastard if you stand around there like a fart in a trance, man?'

With fumbling fingers, the other orderly threaded the curved surgical needle while von Dodenburg, Schulze and his running mate, Matz, watched in horrified fascination. The bald-headed old officer who lay moaning in the vomit and blood on the floor of his office belonged to the signals section of the War Office. After General Fellgiebel, the head of staff signals had killed himself, Skorzeny had ordered the old man's arrest immediately. Why, von Dodenburg didn't know. But as soon as the thugs from the Prinz Albrechtstrasse had appeared, the old man had crunched the lethal pill hidden in his false teeth at the back of his mouth. Now the doctor, the back of his shirt wet with sweat, was working all out to prevent the cyanide from reaching his guts and killing him.

Schulze grunted. Next to him Matz took the looted flatman from his lips, he was so shocked. The SS doctor had pulled out the dying man's tongue. Now he was piercing the organ.

'Holy strawsack,' Matz gasped, letting the precious *Kognak* from the flatman dribble down the side of his slack mouth, 'what's the sawbones up to?'

Von Dodenburg was in no mood to answer. He didn't like what was happening

37

here this bloody July night one bit, though he had no sympathy with the high-level traitors ... if that was what they really were. After all, they were not only betraying the Führer (who could well look after himself) but the poor old stubble-hoppers at the front; the lousy, half-starved poor bastards who were holding the line against the Ivans who outnumbered them at least three to one.

Schulze, however, answered for him. 'Ain't yer got eyes?' he snarled at Matz. 'They're trying to keep the bastard's tongue curled backwards. Stop him swallowing.' He winced too, now, as the sweating medic started to draw the curved needle with its black thread through the coated tongue, as the dying man writhed and twisted on the floor. 'Hey, gimme a swig o' that firewater, Matz. *Quick*! ... I need a shot tootsweet.' He grabbed the flatman and took a greedy gulp at the fiery German brandy.

Von Dodenburg would dearly have loved to have done the same. But he knew he couldn't. It wouldn't look good.

Five minutes later the ordeal was over and the weary MO was pulling the broken pieces of the sugar-coated pill from the old man's throat, while the orderly slapped him across the face, crying, 'Come on, you bastard. Don't try to shit me, traitor. Wake up ... you ain't dead, old man ... *yet*!'

A little while later, just after Skorzeny's men had shot the last bunch of traitors in the courtyard – the dead slumped on the blood-stained cobbles like a confused heap of abandoned rags, stinking, the lot of them, because they had evacuated their bowels in their death agonies – von Dodenburg was summoned to Skorzeny's temporary office.

Seated at the desk in the centre of the room was a dead general, held upright still by some strange force of nature. He had shot himself and the bullet had blown out most of the front of his face. Someone had placed a handkerchief over it. But the cloth had slipped to reveal two pink suppurating pits where his eyes had been. They still oozed blood. On the sofa in the corner, there was his secretary in the grey uniform of the *blitzmädchen* of the signal corps. She had taken poison, von Dodenburg guessed, for her pretty face was suffused with blood and a violent red. In her death agonies, she had writhed back and forth on the leather sofa so that her uniform skirt had ridden up above her stockinged, trim thighs to reveal her pubic hair and the fact that she had not been wearing knickers. Von Dodenburg, who took his eyes away from the awful sight hastily, couldn't imagine why.

'Pretty rotten mess,' Skorzeny commented, as he opened yet another drawer. The floor of the big office was littered with official documents and papers.

When von Dodenburg didn't answer, Skorzeny, who had obviously been drinking – the former could smell the drink on his breath even at that distance – added, 'We're finding the stuff we're looking for.'

'To prove their part in the plot?' von Dodenburg heard himself say; it was as if he were listening to a stranger speaking a long way off.

'Yes, and more.' Skorzeny pulled out his flatman – a silver hip flask – and offered it to the harshly handsome regimental commander of Wotan. The latter shook his head and Skorzeny took a hefty swig of whatever the flatman contained. He shuddered. He wiped his big paw across his scarred, twisted mouth. 'There's a lot more to this bad business than the attempt on the Führer's life.'

'How do you mean, Skorzeny?'

Skorzeny was not a particularly careful man. Indeed, by nature he was a loud mouth and a blusterer. Now, however, he cocked his big head to one side and inspected von Dodenburg slowly, as if he were asking himself whether he could trust the commander of SS Wotan. The look annoyed von Dodenburg. It was just one more affront added to the manifold ones of the last twenty-four hours. Here he was, an 'old hare', a combat soldier who had rushed from the crumbling front in France in order to bolster up the line with whatever 'bodies' he could find in Berlin, involved in the miserable treachery and double-dealing of these 'rear echelon stallions'. 'Come on, Skorzeny,' he urged angrily. 'Piss or get off the pot!' For once he didn't mind the crude old soldier's expression he had probably learned from the notably foul-mouthed Schulze.

Skorzeny's pale face flushed a little and his eyes lit up angrily for a moment. Von Dodenburg could see why the Viennese giant must have been a frightening opponent on the duelling floor with his masked face and sabre raised above his head. Then the angry light went and he said, 'We've caught most of the treacherous swine, as you can see, von Dodenburg. But there are others. They are the most dangerous ... the ones we don't know about.'

'How do you mean?'

'An example?' Skorzeny said with sudden apparent carefulness, and for a fleeting instant von Dodenburg wondered if he, too, wasn't altogether trusted. Perhaps no one was at this moment of supreme crisis. All the same, the thought angered him. '*Yes!*' he urged.

'Well, Field Marshal von Kluge has been recalled from the French battlefield to answer some questions on this business to the Führer.'

The information caught von Dodenburg by surprise. 'The Commander-in-Chief in the West!' he gasped.

Skorzeny nodded solemnly. 'Yes, the traitors seem to be everywhere. In Paris, Brussels ... all the headquarters in the west ... where they can betray our cause to the Anglo-Americans.'

'You mean sue for peace? Is that what you think von Kluge is up to, Skorzeny?'

'Yes.'

Outside they were carrying the old signals officer out to the waiting ambulance on a door wrenched from one of the offices. The sweating medical officer was shooting a hypodermic into his skinny arm, while the orderly continued to slap their victim's face. Obviously they were working hard to keep him alive and a glum, shocked von Dodenburg knew why. So they could get him into the torture cellars of Number Ten Prinz Albrechtstrasse. 'Shit on the shingle,' he cursed to himself, 'what a mess!' His whole world seemed to be falling down about his ears and there didn't appear to be one thing he could do about it.

'Last week he disappeared completely for over a day. Said he had gone to the front to visit the troops,' Skorzeny continued, and his lips twisted contemptuously. 'A damned lie if there ever was one. Where had he gone?' He answered his own question again,

'To talk surrender to the Tommies – that Field Marshal Sir Montgomery of theirs.'

'But that's impossible ... totally out of the question,' von Dodenburg stuttered wildly. 'A German Field Marshal negotiating with the enemy...'

'*Anything* and *everything* is possible these days, von Dodenburg,' Skorzeny interrupted him, dark eyes flashing angrily. 'We cannot trust anyone.' He lowered his voice. 'Now I wish to thank you for your assistance in this matter ... it's been a very bad business. And I don't think it has ended yet. We shall have need of you and your brave chaps of SS Wotan once you have completed your task at the front in France.'

Inwardly von Dodenburg breathed a sigh of relief. At least the powers that be weren't going to keep him in this Berlin madhouse; he was going to be able to return to the cleaner air of the front. Still, he was curious. 'How do you mean, Skorzeny,' he asked, cautious now, for it seemed to him that even a patriotic, loyal German no longer dared to wear his heart on his sleeve. He had to be careful, very careful, with his words. 'You will need me and my regiment in the future?'

'Look at it like this. Who can we trust any more, especially among these rear echelon stallions here in Berlin and other rear headquarters throughout Europe? Senior officers who have grown rich and famous through this war and by the Führer's grace and kindness.' He lowered his voice to a conspiratorial whisper. 'There's even talk of Rommel himself, but no matter.' He swept his big right paw through the air like an irate schoolmaster might wipe off an obscenity chalked on the blackboard by a naughty schoolboy. 'But we do know that even high-ranking generals from our own SS are – *were*,' he corrected himself hastily, crooking his right forefinger as if pulling the trigger of a pistol, 'members of this dastardly conspiracy. Therefore, my dear fellow, we need someone like you. A dedicated National Socialist, experienced at the front, who is in command of troops, who will obey the slightest order without question or hesitation.'

At the door Sergeant Schulze – who was unofficially standing guard on his beloved CO, machine pistol slung around his bull-like neck at the ready – raised his right haunch and farted very slowly.

But such irony was wasted on the giant Austrian. He stuck out his hand. 'Obersturmbannführer, I wish you all the best in France. I shall be in touch. Never fear.' With that he touched his hand to his big cap and stalked out. There was more of his bloody handiwork to be carried out before dawn, that was obvious.

For a moment or two von Dodenburg didn't speak. Even the normally ebullient Schulze standing on guard at the door was unusually quiet for him. Finally the young commander broke the heavy silence. 'All right, you big rogue. Let's see you move those brittle bones of yours.'

Schulze's honest, ruddy face broke into a smile. He was always happy when the CO was. 'Just give the orders, sir,' he snapped.

'Lehrter Station,' von Dodenburg commanded, trying not to look at the secretary with the naked loins. 'We're going home!'

Schulze nodded his understanding. 'Home to the fighting front, sir. Things are simple there.'

'That they are, Schulze,' von Dodenburg said reflectively. 'Shitting simple.'

A minute later they were gone, leaving the corpses of that house of death to stiffen in the dawn cold...

# Death on a Distant Frontier

# September 15 1944

# One

The whole front was on the move. Up on the left flank the infantry were wading through the shallows of River Ourthe while the artillery covered their progress. Up on the heights in Belgium, the 105s of the US 4th Infantry were firing directly into the Reich for the very first time. Behind them the Shermans and the tank destroyers waited for their order to move and provide the support. And to left and right lining the wooded river bank were the waiting boxlike ambulances, their drivers smoking moodily, saying little, just watching the shells bursting in the bunkers of the Siegfried Line beyond. All was noise and controlled confusion, the music of battle.

Colonel 'Buck' Lanham of the Fourth closed his map case firmly and looked around at his officers, 'Well, gentlemen, this is it. At last we're attacking into Krautland.' He saw the earnest look on the officers' faces and he could guess only too well what thoughts were going through their minds at this very moment. He waited till a salvo of huge 105mm shells had burst in a flash of cherry-red flame and deafening sound in 'dead man's gulch' and bellowed, ''Kay, gentlemen, let's go and get the chicken-shitters.' Without waiting to see if they were following he clambered up the fresh brown soil of the shellhole where the last briefing had just taken place and, drawing his .45, set off behind the first line of infantry.

They advanced in a single line, well spread out with their bayonetted rifles at the high port. They moved slowly and thoughtfully across the field of autumn corn like farm labourers at the end of a long hard day. Their bodies were bent forward slightly. They might well have been advancing against a stiff wind. But there was no wind. It was in their anxious minds. To their front the smoke from the shell bursts rose stiffly, straight up into the hard blue of the September sky.

Each man seemed wrapped in a cocoon of his own thoughts and apprehensions. Their bodies were tensed waiting for the first hard thwack of a slug striking their soft flesh. None came. The German bunkers remained silent. There was no reaction even when one of the square pillboxes received a direct hit and great chunks of grey concrete flew everywhere through the still air. It was as if every last German had vanished, was already dead, had fled.

Colonel Lanham, slight and old in comparison with his young soldiers, knew differently. The Krauts were there all right. They'd be behind their steel-and-concrete shields, sweating, damp fingers on the triggers of their machine guns, hearts beating furiously, waiting for the order to open fire. Yes, the Krauts were in place. He raised his voice above the roar of the American guns, echoing and re-echoing around the circle of hills surrounding the battlefield. 'Keep on going, men ... Ain't much longer now ... Keep...'

The rest of his words were drowned by the harsh, high, hysterical burst of machine gun fire. There was no mistaking that weapon. The Kraut GIs called it 'the Hitler Saw'; it was their MG 42, which could easily fire 1,000 rounds a minute. Now one of the damned Nazi machine guns was zeroing in on his first line of infantry. He could see slugs whipping off the heads of the corn in a golden rain and hear the rasp of the bullets cutting the air. In a second, it would reach his infantry.

It did. Suddenly, startlingly, his first line were galvanised into violent, hectic action. They were like a bunch of puppets being worked by a puppet master who had suddenly gone nuts. Their limbs twitched. They whirled round. They screamed. They threw their bloody hands to the sky. They thrashed the corn. They fell, drowning in their own blood. In a flash the first line almost disappeared save for a handful of confused men, who stopped abruptly and stared about like lost travellers looking for a signpost to tell them which way to go.

'Holy shit!' Lanham cried. 'Keep going, goddam you ... *keep going!*' Furiously he blew a blast on his whistle and slammed his fist down hard on his helmet, then jerked it up and down three times. It was the infantry signal for 'rally on me ... double time'. As if to emphasise the urgency of the moment, the little infantry colonel yelled, beside himself with rage, face scarlet, 'Come on you bastards ... Do you want to fucking live for ever?'

Behind him his company officers shrilled blasts on their whistles too. Burly noncoms yelled. Others booted the backsides of reluctant GIs. The second line started to move through the carpet of their own dead to the attack.

The little colonel felt a sense of pride surge through his wiry skinny body. A feeling of hope, too. Surely the Krauts wouldn't be able to stop such brave men? God couldn't be that unfair. Men who braved such a hail of fire could not but succeed in attaining their objective.

Colonel Lanham was wrong. God *was* unfair this September morning. Now machine guns had opened up from both flanks. The advancing infantry were caught in a lethal crossfire. Men went down everywhere, gasping their last breaths. Hastily the mortar crews sprang into action. Without waiting for orders, they fired. There was the obscene whang and bang of 3-inch mortars opening up. Ugly round bombs fell out of the sky. Right on top of the German positions. Thick plumes of ugly black smoke went up on both flanks. To no avail. The Kraut gunners were hidden deep in their concrete bunkers. Even direct hits couldn't affect them. Still the SS machine-gunners kept up the slaughter. The second line seemed to melt away. In front of the little colonel what appeared to be a khaki-and-red carpet had abruptly been spread across the crushed corn.

Colonel Lanham shook his fist at the lowering, smoke-drifting sky, as if cursing God himself. Still he kept going, firing his pistol uselessly while the third and last line of infantry caught up with him.

Now, however, their courage was draining out of them rapidly. It was as if someone had opened an unseen tap. Lanham could hear it in their hectic, panicked breathing, the furious obscene swearing, the meaningless cries against their fate. Still they kept on. Discipline and pride in the Regiment had not yet broken. He knew it would.

Soon. Now they were only a few yards from their objective. He had to keep them going. Rush it and they'd swing the damned thing.

'At the double,' he yelled against the hollow boom of the mortar bombs exploding and the high-pitched burr of the Kraut machine guns. 'Come on ... let's get them frigging chickenshitters. Come on boys ... *For the sake of the old twenty-second!*'

Then the German fire smashed into them at point-blank range. Hastily Lanham shoved another magazine into his Colt. Standing there, with men falling and dying on both sides of him in the cornfield, he fired deliberately, as if back on some peacetime range at Benning or Bliss. Shot after shot at the nearest bunker. He could see the slugs kick up fiery purple sparks and grey eruptions of concrete dust as they struck home.

This was the sort of stuff they had taught him back at West Point as a kid in the '20s. It was supposed to win battles. But not now. Not here. The machine guns firing a thousand rounds a minute were not impressed by personal bravery. What he needed – what the Regiment needed – were tanks, Bangalore torpedoes, satchel charges and the like. All they had, though, were soft bodies and M-1 rifles.

Next to him a kid was hit. He screamed. But stayed on his feet. His rifle fell from nerveless fingers. Still he didn't go down, as the scarlet patch started to spread with slow inexorability across the front of his khaki shirt. Instead, his hands clawed the air, as if he were climbing the rungs of an invisible ladder. Why? To where? Lanham didn't know ... never found out.

Suddenly the kid gave a groan which seemed to come from the bottom of his heart, one of unbelievable despair. Without another sound, the kid pitched face-forward into the trampled corn, dead before he hit the ground.

That seemed to do it. It was as if a signal had been given. The men faltered. For a moment the Krauts ceased firing, as if they were considering whether they should waste any more precious ammunition on these Amis, who were already defeated even if they didn't know it yet. Distinctly Lanham heard somebody say, 'I need a shit, Joe.'

Then the Regiment broke.

One moment the men were still struggling forward, hopping and climbing over the already dead, faces grim, set and determined. The next they were reeling back, some already breaking into a stumbling run, thrashing through the corn, eyes wide and wild like those of men demented. Meaningless sounds came from their lips. Others cried obscenities... *'no fucking use ... We didn't have a frigging chance ... Kraut cunts ... machine guns everywhere...'* It was as if the 'manly' cusswords would absolve them of all charges of cowardice. Here and there, men threw away their rifles openly, not caring what their comrades thought. Others grabbed the walking wounded, yelling *'Medic ... over here for Chrissake ... this guy's hit!'*

Desperately, tears of rage and sorrow streaming down his blanched face, Colonel Lanham tried to stop them. 'Stand fast,' he yelled... 'For Pete's sake, guys, stand fast!' He held his arms spread like a kid in the schoolyard, playing some 'catch' game. To no avail. The men were beyond reason and fear of punishment. They brushed by the lone colonel, swinging him round with the impact, leaving him alone with the already dead and those who soon would be. The 22nd Infantry Regiment's first attack on the Siegfried Line had ended in total, absolute failure.

Up in the steeple of Brandscheid's hilltop church, Obersturmbannführer Kuno von Dodenburg surveyed the fleeing Amis. He felt neither joy at his own victory, nor sorrow at the loss of so many fellow human beings on the American side. The young SS Colonel had seen so many battlefields these last five years that he no longer cared much for his fellow human beings, friend or foe. His sole interest, it seemed, was SS Assault Regiment Wotan. The Regiment was his home, his fatherland, his family. He lowered his glasses. Next to him Schulze said, 'The Amis have taken their hindlegs into their hands, eh, sir?'

Von Dodenburg nodded. 'Yes, they're running.'

'Be some nice pickings down there, sir,' Schulze hinted pointedly. 'You know what rich bastards them Yanks are. Fags, chocolate, perhaps even a little firewater for my bad chest.' He coughed weakly, as if in the last stages of galloping consumption.

'Come off it, Schulze,' von Dodenburg said, as the men in the bunkers ceased firing, leaving behind a loud echoing silence that seemed to go on for ever. 'You and your bad chest ... you're pulling my pisser.'

'It's not the kind of language we of the NCO corps expect from our officers, sir ... pulling the...' He stopped short. He could see the CO was no longer listening.

Instead he had picked up his glasses again and was focusing them hastily on the Belgian side of the River Ourthe. Out of the side of his mouth he ordered, 'Schulze, ten o'clock ... Those staff cars ... next to the group of shot away firs ... got it?'

Rapidly Schulze followed the officer's instructions, as, down below, smoke shells started to land with soft plops in the cornfield, exploding and releasing thick brown smoke to cover the retreat of the enemy survivors. He swung his own glasses to the left. Three long khaki-clad Packards slipped into the shining, calibrated circles of his binoculars. Hastily he adjusted the instrument. The image became clear. Around the saloon cars there was a circle of jeeps. They were packed with white-helmeted Amis. 'White mice,' Schulze said. He meant American military policemen whose helmets and equipment were a pure white.

'Yes. But look in the middle of the circle, you big rogue,' von Dodenburg said, not taking his eyes off the little scene among the trees on the other side of the border for one instant. 'Generals ... Ami generals.' He grinned, but there was nothing pleasant about that grin. His face remained as ruthless and as aggressive as ever. 'You know, Schulze, I've captured French generals, Greek generals, bags of Russian ones, even a British general once ... all baggy shorts and buck teeth ... But never an Ami one ... *yet!*'

Now it was Schulze's turn to grin. 'I read you sir...' he chuckled hugely. 'I read you loud and clear, sir...'

# Two

'Bad show, Tubby,' Eisenhower said, using one of those English expressions he had picked up over the last year or so in London. He held out his hand to General 'Tubby' Barton, Commander of the 4th US Infantry Division. 'But,' he shrugged, 'I guess it's one of those things.'

Barton, big and beefy, looking even bigger in his heavy trenchcoat, was obviously embarrassed. It wasn't every day that you had the Supreme Commander come personally to the front to watch a regimental-sized infantry attack. 'I'm sorry, sir. But we did our best. We'll have another go ... as soon as Colonel Lanham reforms his command.'

'I'm sure you will,' Eisenhower agreed without enthusiasm. The September sun was setting behind the ridgeline to the west and it was getting colder. He wanted the warmth of the big Packard. Besides his 'football knee' was giving him hell again.

Barton saluted. Eisenhower returned the salute smartly, as if they were both cadets back at the Point. Then he hobbled swiftly back to the car, where Kay Summersby, the green-eyed Englishwoman who was his driver – and other things, too – was waiting impatiently and looking worried. Swiftly she opened the door and whispered out of the side of her narrow, rather cruel-looking mouth, 'As soon as we get going, Ike, put that rug over your legs and keep your knee warm.' He nodded and wondered again how an old crock like himself could be attractive to such a pretty woman, and an ex-model to boot.

Behind the Supreme Commander's car the others formed up with a jeep packed with tommy-gun-armed MPs in front and behind each Packard. Standing in the ditches and outside their khaki tents, the cooks and orderlies of the Fourth watched in silence, while the engineers rebuilding the hilltop road rested on their shovels and watched insolently, as if challenging the Brass to reprimand them.

Eisenhower had never commanded even a platoon in action in his thirty-year-long Army career, yet he knew the signs. It was called by the British 'dumb insolence'. The men were showing what they thought of the fat cats of the Army's Brass. But this was not the time or place to take up the challenge. He had to get back to Versailles before it got really dark and he had a couple of appointments in nearby Luxembourg before then. So he contented himself with waving at the troops and smiling that famous ear-to-ear smile of his that was now known throughout the free world. It didn't matter that he got no response from the sullen men of the Fourth. It did the job.

Slowly, the exhaust fumes clouding on the cool forest air, the convoy set off up the incline. They'd drive down the long and dangerous road to Luxembourg, which ran along the frontier with Germany, and hope they'd reach their destination before it was completely dark. For there had been dark tales bandied about among the headquarters drivers of vehicles disappearing from what the GIs called – predictably – 'Skyline Drive'. It was rumoured that since the US Army had reached this distant frontier, chasing the fleeing and broken Wehrmacht before it, the German resistance had solidified and now the Krauts were sending over 'snatch parties' to bushwhack lone US vehicles. Hence the twenty or so MP jeeps escorting the present convoy.

Ike yawned, pulled the plaid rug over his knees as Kay had ordered, and settled back in the plush seat of the big Packard. He'd grab a half-hour's shut-eye before they reached General Bradley's HQ in Luxembourg City...

Schulze waved his right arm cautiously. Behind him on the wooded slope that led to the N51, running from St Vith to Weiswampach in Luxembourg, the young panzer grenadiers in their camouflaged jackets crouched hastily. They, too, could now hear the faint hum of vehicles to the north.

Schulze gave a grunt and said to Matz crouched next to him, 'All right, you Bavarian barnshitter, do you think you can make it with that peg leg of yours, eh?'

'Leg! If you say another word, I'll stick it so far up yer keester, Schulze, that your frigging eyes'll pop out!'

Schulze was in no way offended. He grinned. For his mind was full of the Ami goodies that should be coming their way this evening if everything went well. 'All right, don't piss yerself, Matzi. Just asking. See that shot-up Ferdinand over there on the other side of the road?'

'See it? I don't need a frigging white stick yet, you know!'

Schulze ignored the comment. 'I'll stretch the wire to that. Once I give you the signal, you pull it tight. Then we're in business.'

'Poor shit,' Matz said thoughtfully, rubbing his unshaven chin, 'he's gonna have a nasty headache, don't yer think, Schulzi.'

'War, old house, blame it on the war.' Now Schulze was businesslike. 'All right, keep me covered. Here I go!' With that he was up and running at the double across the main highway towards the shot-up German self-propelled gun. For such a big man he was fast and almost noiseless. Still, his old running mate Matz kept a watchful eye on him as the big NCO dropped into the ditch on the opposite side of the ridge road. For a moment he remained hidden there. Then, presumably knowing the coast was clear, Schulze set about securing the cable around the rear bogey of the big German SP.

Behind Matz the troop of young panzer grenadiers began to take up their positions. They were all new recruits straight from the Berlin depot. They were obviously excited by this first taste of action and, Matz told himself scornfully, the greenhorns would soon be smiling on the other side of their pretty mugs, once the shit really started flying.

Now they waited.

The noise of motor engines negotiating the curves in the ridge road became louder. Schulze tensed. He could make out the roar of a motorbike coming closer. He cursed. He knew instinctively that any motorcycle outrider could not help but see the cable even if it lay in the mud and grime of the road's surface. After all, that was what the rider's job probably was, to spot any potentially dangerous obstacles. What was he going to do?

Now he could hear the racket the rider made as he changed down to take the steep bend ahead. Schulze felt the cold sweat of tension trickling unpleasantly down the small of his back. He had only a matter of moments to make a decision. What in the name of Christ was that going to be?

In the same instant that the helmeted figure, with his goggles raised, came round the bend, glancing suspiciously to left and right, he had. He acted. Snatching out his pistol, he fired a quick burst of tracer to his rear. The white tracer slashed the evening gloom in a deadly morse. The driver braked. Next second, he whirled his bike round. It sprang over the drainage ditch. It slammed into the slight embankment, wobbled dangerously and then the driver had regained control and was leaning down close to the handlebars, going all out for where he supposed that surprising burst of automatic fire had come from. 'Bye, bye, little birdie,' Schulze chortled, highly pleased with himself. His smile vanished as soon as it had appeared. The first jeep had nosed its way cautiously around the bend, the three 'white mice' eyeing the terrain to both sides of the ridge road in that suspicious manner of military policemen around the world.

Hastily, Schulze ducked behind the wrecked self-propelled gun. He peered through the gleaming silver hole skewered through its armour by an armour-piercing anti-tank shell. He said a swift prayer the Amis wouldn't stop to examine the wrecked vehicle. They didn't. The jeep rolled on. Moments later it had disappeared behind the next bend and the first of the big staff cars, metal flags flying on its bonnet, appeared. 'Big shots,' Schulze told himself and ducked again. This one he'd let go by. It was the last one of the convoy he was after for the chief. The Packard might only contain an inferior general, perhaps some humble quartermaster. All the same he *was* a general.

Thus the Allied Supreme Commander, General Eisenhower – commander of some five million soldiers – passed by safely, snug and warm under his plaid rug, mouth open and snoring lightly. Another staff car passed ten seconds or so later. The generals were observing regular convoy distances, Schulze noted. But then, he told himself, the big shots wrote the rules; hell, they'd better observe them.

Now he forgot the others. The last of the motorcycle outriders had gone. That meant they'd be coming to the last of the convoy. Another jeep, then the staff car, and that would be that. The time for action had come. He gripped the cable more firmly in his big paws. Despite the evening coldness his palms were damp. Nerves. He sniffed and sneered at himself, 'You'll be wetting your knickers, darling.' He blew a wet kiss at the growing darkness. Behind him he heard the sound of the lone motorbike cop dying away. Obviously he had rejoined the convoy further up the road. He was out of the way. Now he could concern himself wholly with what was to come. He said a little prayer – or what passed for a prayer in the Schulze family, devoted to sex, suds and sudden mayhem as their only form of religion – and started to tug the cable a little tighter. At the other side of the road, Matz in charge of the greenhorns was doing the same. *So far so good*, Schulze told himself.

Now he could hear the grunt and crash as the driver of the still unseen jeep changed down to take the trigger bend. He tugged the cable sharply. It was his signal. At the other end Matz did the same an instant later. He'd understood. They were ready.

Schulze tensed. Next moment the lone jeep came round the bend, its tyres splattering mud to left and right. Obviously the driver was being slow and careful; the road would appear greasy, slick and dangerous to him. The little vehicles, as Schulze knew, would overturn at the drop of a hat. There were three 'white mice' in it: driver, guard next to him – machine pistol slung round his neck – and another Ami in the back seat and apparently asleep. Clearly they were expecting trouble, however, for the white mice, huddled in their parkas, had pulled down the windscreen as the Amis always did when they anticipated trouble. That way, if they were hit, they wouldn't be blinded by flying glass splinters. The sight cheered Schulze up considerably. It was just what he had hoped for.

A second afterwards the Packard saloon came round the bend, going slow in third gear too. Behind it there was nothing. It was the end of the convoy. Hastily, not taking his gaze off the two unsuspecting vehicles for one moment, Schulze started to count off the seconds. Now the jeep driver had changed up. The road ahead was straight and he started to pick up speed. Perhaps with the falling darkness, he did not want to fall too far behind the others. Whatever his motive, it was the worst thing he could possibly have done now.

'Six ... *five* ... *four* ... *three*...'

The jeep was less than twenty metres off now, '...*two*...' Even in the poor evening light, with the fog starting to curl in and out of the damp firs like a silent soft grey cat, Schulze could see every detail of the little vehicle and its occupants '...*one*!' Schulze waited no longer. A tug. *Hard*. His brutal shoulder muscles swelled up under the strain. They threatened to burst out of his tunic. The cable came up as required, splattering mud and leaves everywhere. For a moment the jeep driver was transfixed with horror. His face contorted, he didn't react. It was fatal. Even as he attempted to wrench the wheel to the right, the cable slammed into his neck. He gave a shrill scream like a hysterical woman. It was cut off the next moment, as the steel cable sliced cruelly through the soft flesh. His head, complete with white helmet, was sheered off cleanly. The head rolled towards the ditch, like a football abandoned by some careless schoolkid. Out of control, with the headless driver slumped over the controls and the man in the back screaming help-lessly, the jeep went over the side, slithering and sliding, bits and pieces trailing behind it in a metallic rain, heading for the river far below.

But the ambushers had no time for the jeep. The saloon car was almost upon them. Automatically Schulze noted the one star of a brigadier-general on the left side of the front bumper. That pleased him. The CO would be getting his Ami general as plan-ned. He raised his machine pistol and aimed at the right side front tyre. He pressed the trigger. *Click!* Nothing happened. He cursed and pressed again. Once more, nothing. 'Great frigging balls of fire,' he cursed in an almost unbearable agony of rage. 'A frigging stoppage!'

The American sergeant next to the driver reacted quicker than Schulze anticipated. As the driver ran through his gears frantically, obviously trying to get reverse and back out of the ambush, he leaned out of the window and fired without aiming.

The slug whined off the side of the wrecked self-propelled gun, less than half a metre from Schulze's head. 'Fuck this for a game o' soldiers!' he cried in alarm. Hastily he fumbled with the side of his left jackboot. He pulled out the stick grenade he had stuck down it. In one and the same movement, he ripped open the pin and flung the grenade. It whirled through the air as, on the other side of the road, Matz took up the challenge, peppering the side of the big olive-green Packard with bullets from his Schmeisser machine pistol. The white star of the Allied armies painted on the door disappeared in that furious hail. Next instant Schulze's stick grenade exploded in a fury of red flame.

The sedan came up on the rear axle like a wild west bucking bronco. The front hovered there for what seemed a long time. Then it came crashing down. The axle shattered. Both tyres exploded and went limp. The windscreen cracked into a gleaming spider's web of shattered glass. As steam started to pour from the ruptured engine and the occupants of the ambushed car disappeared from view, Matz and his young greenhorns surmounted the rise behind which they had been hidden and rushed the car. '*Alles für Deutschland*!' The old fearsome rallying cry of the SS, which had put the fear of God into so many of their foes, rang out. But it was not necessary. As the first greedy blue flames of leaking petrol started to lick about the shattered engine, there was no return fire from inside the car.

With surprising speed for a one-legged man, Matz wrenched open the door to the passenger seat and levelled his machine pistol. '*Halt! Hände hoch!*' he cried, too excited by the thrill and bloodlust of action to realise that at that moment he was speaking to an American.

But the Ami reacted. The little officer, who looked more like a civilian poured into a general's uniform – hurriedly at that – raised his pale, well-manicured hands and said in flawless German, '*Bitte, nicht schiessen ... Ich mache kein Ärger* ... Please, don't shoot...'

While Matz recovered from his surprise and jerked the muzzle of his machine pistol forward to indicate that the man should get out – it would be only a matter of moments before the engine exploded – the others pulled out the two NCOs in the front and grabbed whatever goodies they could lay their greedy hands on.

Five minutes later they were rushing their

prisoners down the steep slope to the River Ourthe below, with Schulze chortling happily between greedy slugs of the flask of bourbon they had found in their prisoner's pocket, 'He ain't much of a general ... but he's the only one we've got...'

# Three

Solemnly the Supreme Commander's car drew up in front of the Hotel Alpha, opposite Luxembourg's Gare Principale. The two immaculate sentries clicked to attention and the Luxembourgers all around, fat, flat-faced, prosperous burghers, raised their hats in salutation.

General Bradley, the Commander of the US 12th Army Group, came clattering down the steps to meet his boss and old West Point friend. For some reason, although he had just come down from his quarters on the second floor of the old, turn-of-the-century hotel, he was wearing a burnished steel helmet adorned with the three stars of a lieutenant-general.

His homely face broke into a smile and his eyes twinkled behind his steel-rimmed GI glasses, 'Welcome to Luxembourg, sir!' He saluted.

Eisenhower returned it for the sake of the observers and shook Bradley's hand. 'Relax, Brad,' he said warmly. 'Good to see you again, old friend!'

Then his smile vanished. 'Let's go inside, Brad, I need a drink.' He flashed a quick look at Kay Summersby. She gave the Supreme Commander a slight nod, as if in approval. Then without another look at him, she moved off at the order of the 'white mouse' directing traffic. Brad saw the exchange of looks but said nothing. Eisenhower had looked after him well these last months: from brigadier-general to three star rank. He was not about to rock the boat over a dame.

Together they passed into the lobby of the old hotel, which smelled of beef tartare and ancient lecheries, as most of these one night stands around the city's central station did. Bradley nodded to the military waiter and held up two fingers. The waiter understood. The gesture meant two whiskies, the only drink in the place that was in short supply. You could drink bourbon, cognac, champagne, even Kraut schnapps by the gallon. But not Scotch whisky.

They sat down and Bradley waited till the special drinks arrived, noting how glum Ike looked. It wasn't just his wretched knee, which he had hurt as a young rookie at West Point and which still gave him trouble. It was something else. Ike took a deep gulp of the rationed whisky and gave an appreciative, grateful nod in Bradley's direction. 'Thanks, Brad. That was a life-saver.'

'You're welcome, Ike.'

But already Ike's brief grin had vanished again as he continued, 'As you know, I went up to see Tubby Barton's outfit this morning. You know, the armoured and infantry reconnaissance into Germany which I agreed with you and the Army Group in Chartres two weeks ago.'

Bradley nodded and savoured the good Scotch whisky. He said nothing. Outside, a couple of staff officers – Ivy League, Bradley thought, by the sound of them – were discussing an invitation to the Grand Duchess's castle for cocktails. Should they wear Class A uniforms for the occasion and what was the correct form of address for a grand duchess. Brad shook his head. Some of his staff seemed to have forgotten that the Krauts were only twenty miles up the road and that there was a war going on; he'd have to mention it at the next staff conference.

'It was a total failure,' Ike was saying. 'The guys of the Fourth did their best. They tried to take their objective more than once and they paid the butcher's bill – and then some – in trying. But in the end those damned Kraut fortifications stopped them.' His face was abruptly very bitter. 'I don't care what the papers and the pundits back home say about the Siegfried Line being defended by kids and old men, but any old prick with one eye is still better than the keenest young infantryman as long as he's protected by three foot of reinforced steel.'

Bradley was a little shocked by Ike's choice of language. He wasn't given to using words like 'old prick'. But it was a sign of his boss's anger and resentment against the armchair strategists back home. 'Another snort, Ike?' he asked, as Eisenhower finished his drink with a flourish.

The Supreme Commander shook his head. 'No thanks, Brad. I've got to keep my wits about me now. You see, there are not going to be any easy victories here on this goddam frontier. We all thought that when they made that attempt on Hitler's life last July that the Jerries were done for. It was all over bar the shouting. We even had contact with the German High Command. There were problems. They wanted to surrender to us but not to our allies the Russians.' He shook his head at the memory. 'But I'm sure we could have ironed it out in time, working together with Uncle Joe.' Eisenhower meant the Soviet dictator, Josef Stalin. 'But it didn't work out, as you well know, Brad.'

General Bradley nodded. He could tell that Ike was feeling the strain. First the almost unbearable burden of D-Day. Now this frustration on the Kraut frontier. It was really too much for one man to bear. 'It'll work out, Ike,' he attempted to console the Supreme Commander. 'They're running out of bodies up there at the front.'

'No, they aren't. Strong, my chief of intelligence, tells me they've got the remnants of four SS armoured divisions facing your 1st Army, plus half a dozen other ad hoc formations, Brad. And remember this: they have got the cover of those goddam Siegfried Line fortifications. Hell, the British were gonna hang out their washing on them back in '39,' he added bitterly, 'and they still haven't done so.'

'But that's the British. We're the Yanks, Ike.'

The Supreme Commander ignored the remark. Outside, there was the muted sound of clapping and cheering, drowning the rattle and clatter of the battered Luxembourg City trams.

'But what about your contacts with these guys of the German High Command?'

'Most of them are dead by now ... and I think I'll have another drink after all, Brad, if you don't mind.'

'Sure, Ike.' Hastily Bradley rose and started to refill their glasses, happy that Eisenhower was at least taking a drink; it might relax him.

'Couldn't you make some sort of approach to those Kraut generals?' he asked, handing Eisenhower his scotch. 'Even if you did it openly, stating you were prepared to discuss terms?'

Eisenhower accepted the drink with a hand that trembled badly. 'Impossible, Brad! One, the President and Mr Churchill have agreed that the only terms we can offer the Krauts, however good their intentions, are unconditional surrender. I could not go behind the backs of the political big shots and tell the Kraut brass that we are prepared to discuss terms. You know that, Brad. My head would be on the line in five minutes flat.' He took a hasty gulp of his scotch and gasped as the strong spirit hit the back of his throat. 'As far as I'm concerned – *officially* – I know nothing of any discussions between us and the German generals.'

Bradley caught that 'officially'. He lowered his glass hastily from his lips, even before he had taken a drink of the scotch. '*Unofficially*, Ike?' he queried, leaning forward, noting the cheering and clapping in the Place de la Gare.

Ike hesitated. He looked hard at his old classmate, as if he were seeing him for the very first time and was trying to assess how trustworthy Bradley was. Finally he said, 'You know that propaganda broadcasting station you've got back there on the hill at ... er...'

'Junglinster,' Bradley supplied the name of the village, some ten miles from where they were at this present moment.

'Yeah. Junglinster. That's where you've got those Jew Krauts sending propaganda to their army facing you.'

'Yes,' Bradley answered promptly, puzzled but proud all the same. 'In fact, even if I do say, Ike, I'm the only army commander in the US Army throughout the world who has his own black propaganda station ... and other things,' he added a little lamely, noting that Eisenhower's mind was elsewhere, a puzzled frown on that high, balding forehead of his.

'I want you to double the guard on that place immediately,' Eisenhower said suddenly. Down below, the noise had ceased now and had been replaced by that of the city traffic.

*'Double?'*

'Yes, Brad. I passed Jung ... er ... Junglinster on the way here coming back from the Fourth and it's pretty isolated up there on the hill. Hell, I'm sure the Krauts can see it from their own lines on the River Sauer on a good day.'

'Agreed. They can, Ike.' Swiftly, glass in hand – whisky was too precious to waste even at Army Group HQ – Bradley walked over to his 'squawk box'. He flipped up the black switch. There was a muffled voice. Without any formalities Bradley snapped, 'Joe, get on to HQ guard commander. Order him to send a fully armed MP com-

78

pany to the old Radio Luxembourg site at Junglinster. He'll know where it is. If he doesn't, he better damned well find out ASAP. I'll explain. Out.' He flipped the switch back again. The static ceased.

'Thanks, Brad,' Eisenhower said. 'We can't be too careful. The Krauts could take that place out as it stands with one hand tied behind their backs. You can't expect those toy soldiers of Kraut Jewboys to be able to defend the place if the chips were down, can you?'

Bradley nodded his agreement, though by now he was completely bewildered. Why in Sam Hill's name, he asked himself, was the Supreme Commander, with eight armies, numbering millions of men under his command, concerning himself with the Junglinster site and the thirty-odd men who ran the broadcasting station on the hill? Still, he kept the question to himself. Ike would enlighten him when he was good and ready. It was his prerogative as Supreme Commander.

'So, as I see it, Brad,' Eisenhower went on – rolling his whisky glass between his hands, as if he were weaving his plan as he spoke, eyes far away – 'we can beat our heads on that goddam Siegfried Line of theirs for weeks, perhaps months, and the bad weather will soon be on us. That won't make operations any easier.'

Bradley nodded his agreement. It certainly wouldn't. He already knew from his met men that once November came up in these hills of the Ardennes, they might well be under snow for weeks. That would put the kybosh on mobile operations, which were the strength of the US Army. The doughs of the infantry had come to rely on air and tanks to cover them when they attacked. In bad weather they'd be none too happy without them.

'So, Brad, we've got to make a breakthrough up there before we start running out of infantry reinforcements. Washington's already squawking that they just don't have the men. They're combing the Army Air Corps and the Coastal Artillery for reinforcements.' He looked hard at Bradley. 'Why, there's even some talk of asking darkies to volunteer for the infantry.'

Bradley looked suitably shocked. In America's segregated army there had not been blacks in US fighting units since the turn of the century and the Spanish-American War.

'Kay, Ike.' Bradley tried to have a go at achieving some kind of clarity. 'What's the new plan? I assume you have one. If we can't get through with what we've got, I guess you've got some cunning scheme up your sleeve to make the breakthrough before the winter snows start falling? I

80

mean, if we're still trying when that happens, we'll have to postpone large-scale ops till the spring of '45 ... and, Ike,' he added, his voice suddenly very serious, 'Joe Public won't like that one bit. Washington could well insist that heads roll out here.'

'You can bet your bottom dollar on that, Brad. And the head that could roll might easily be *mine*!' He finished his drink and leaned forward, lowering his voice as he did so, as if he were afraid that he might be overheard. 'So, we're going to have another go.'

'Another attack on Gerow's Fifth Corps front?'

'No, Brad, I saw enough today with the Fourth Infantry. We can't afford to waste any more riflemen. They're the most precious commodity in Europe at this moment in time. No,' Eisenhower repeated even more firmly, face set as if he had just made his mind up, 'we're gonna...'

He never finished his sentence. For at that exact moment there came a thunderous knock on the door. Even as Bradley cried angrily, 'Come on in for Chrissake!' young Captain Sylvan, his aide-de-camp, did so. His face flushed excitedly and he waved a piece of paper, which turned out to be his 'short snort', a dollar bill on which GIs in the European Theater of Operations collected the signatures of those they encountered

81

and wished to remember.

'*He's here ... He's here ... And he just gave me his autograph!*' he cried.

Ike's well-known ear-to-ear grin, which had endeared him to cinema audiences throughout the Free World, vanished. He looked icily at the young and elegant officer, waving his crumpled dollar bill. It was a look that might well have frozen another officer to a pillar of ice. 'And pray, *who* in the name of hell is here, Captain?'

Sylvan rose to the bait. 'Why, sir, *Major Glenn Miller personally*, sir...' he grinned foolishly, 'and he says he has an urgent appointment with you.'

# London, England
## October 1944

# One

Now the sirens were beginning to sound
their shrill warning. At first they had been
faint, insignificant wails to the east of the
British capital. Now they were running
along the Thames into the centre of London, growing louder and more frightening
by the moment. To the east the guns were
already thundering. But no one believed in
the effectiveness of the anti-aircraft batteries
any more. The deadly new weapons the
enemy was employing were too fast for the
3.7-inch Bofors. Those who were not too
panicked as they headed for the shelters
hoped that the RAF fighter fields had
already scrambled their planes. The new
Spitfires with their supercharged engines
might just be able to attack the deadly
invaders, if they were lucky. And brave
enough, they might have added. For the
only way to really deal with them was to tip
their stub wings and send them hurtling to
the ground before they reached their target
area. But you had to be a damned skilled

pilot with ice-water in your veins to attempt that manoeuvre. One false move and you could be both victor and victim.

Lt Colonel David Niven tapped the ancient cabbie – with the half-smoked Woodbine stuck behind his right ear – on the shoulder and said in that voice familiar to cinema audiences everywhere in America and Britain, 'All right, cabbie, this'll do us, please. We'll walk the rest of the way. Might be safer.'

Obediently, the cabbie pulled up and said, 'Bit different from Hollywood, sir!' He grinned cheerfully and looked at the other passenger, in the uniform of an American major, though with his pasty face and big spectacles, he didn't look much like a soldier. 'Bet you didn't think it'd be like this over here either, sir?'

Glenn Miller grunted something in reply. He was obviously not in a good mood. So the cabbie turned back to Colonel Niven who handed him a pound note and said, 'Keep the change, cabbie, and get yourself off to some shelter before the buggers start dropping.'

'Ta, sir,' the cabbie chortled, happy with the big tip, 'you're a gent. Don't worry, sir, there's worse things at sea.'

'Suppose there are,' Niven agreed, and then they were out and walking close to the buildings lining Wardour Street, hoping they might give shelter just in case. Up front one of the new fangled V-1s' engines stopped. There was a sudden silence and Niven told himself that, if he had been an imaginative man, he would have surmised that half of London was now listening apprehensively for what was soon to come.

A moment later, it did.

A thud. A shudder. A strange moment's silence. Then the ton of high explosive the deadly automaton carried went up. Smoke erupted upwards. Scarlet flame stabbed the October gloom. A wall trembled. The two officers tensed. Next moment the blast whipped them across the face like a blow from a flabby open palm. They gasped for breath. The very air seemed to be dragged from their lungs. Then it was over, and they could hear the slow putt-putt – like the noise made by an ancient two-stroke motorbike – of the next one coming home to wreak Hitler's vengeance on the hard-pressed British capital.

Miller wiped the mess off his big glasses. 'Holy mackerel, David,' he gasped. That was goddam close!'

'Worry about the one you don't hear, old boy,' Niven said in his usual high-pitched jaunty fashion. He brushed the dust off his elegant, immaculate uniform. 'Come on, let's get to the studio before the Huns let us have the benefit of the next one.'

'Christ Almighty,' Miller snapped peevishly in his plaintive mid-western accent, 'why the hell do I have to do this thing, David?'

Niven – his boss – smiled, revealing those beautiful teeth of his. 'As I might have said in "The Charge of the Light Brigade", but fortunately didn't have to – even *I* couldn't have been that trite and corny – "Ours not to reason why ... ours but to do and die" '. His smile broadened even more. 'Ike has commanded, we shall obey...'

Five minutes later they were in the cellars of the recording studio and in relative safety. At least there was a nice warm muted fug about the place which made it feel as if they were well below the earth's surface, proof against whatever an angry Adolf Hitler might be able to throw at them. Perched on the edge of a desk, swinging his elegantly trousered leg above a gleaming shoe, Niven watched the proceedings with a practised, if somewhat bored gaze. While his subordinate went through the motions – earphones cutting out the noise, accompanied by a very pretty German-American, who Niven, the inveterate skirt-chaser, thought might well be worth a sin or two – he, too, considered why Miller had been picked for whatever mission the Yanks had dreamed up for him.

He thought Miller a typical musician-

88

businessman; though, in his experience, an artist who was also capable of wheeling and dealing was a fairly rare breed. He was an excellent trombone player and orchestrator of music in the modern swing fashion. But at the same time he distanced himself from his band members, who – typical of their kind – lived for the day and, when they weren't playing, devoted themselves to what they claimed were 'fast women and slow horses'. As a result they seemed permanently broke, hung-over and, if they were unlucky, sadly afflicted by the diseases concurrent with a life of sexual wickedness. He grinned at the thought of the same kind of life he and Errol had lived in their bachelor years in Hollywood before the war.

Now this bandleader – the darling of the zoot-suiters and boogie-woogie generation – had been picked for a job that up to now had been totally out of his ken. Niven, the veteran of four years of war, wondered yet again at the mind-set of those who commanded the US Army, if that was who was in charge of the operation involving Major Glenn Miller.

He dismissed the thought for a few moments and watched, slightly amused, as Miller struggled with the German commentary that was to go with this new music project. Whoever was behind the plot had provided him with an excellent female aide.

Not only was she sexy, she also seemed pretty smart, if not downright cunning.

When Miller fluffed his pronunciation, she would lean forward provocatively – giving the bespectacled maestro full view of her delightful cleavage – and breathe, 'No, Major Miller, I know you've almost got it, but to be perfect you've got to pronounce the *umlaut* like this, "*Fuenf Uhr Jive*" '; and she'd puff out her splendid breasts and add softly, 'Now that's right. You *do* catch on quick!'

Niven told himself that unfortunately Major Miller wasn't catching on quickly enough. The assistant, Heidi or whatever she was called, was offering herself to him on a silver platter and he didn't realise it. Not that the Yank was any great catch. But Niven guessed she was going to be another watchdog – just as he was himself – to ensure that Miller didn't spill the beans.

By eleven o'clock that morning, with the V-1s still coming over in a steady stream, Miller had recorded the German commentary to 'Five O'Clock Jump' and – naturally – 'In the Mood', when the studio manager called for a coffee break, and Niven could see that Miller needed it. The effort of watching the recordings and talking German told. He looked even more fagged than usual.

Niven offered him the mug of coffee and,

although he pulled a face when he tasted it, muttering something about the 'limeys' not being able to make 'a goddamn cup o' java', he breathed a grateful sigh and said, 'I needed that!'

Niven took out his hip flask. 'Like to liven it up?'

Miller shook his big head. 'Not while I'm working,' he answered.

Niven gave him that cheery, if fake, smile of his and said, 'Quite right, Glenn,' whereupon he took a hefty snort himself straight from the flask. At the other end of the studio the aide had pulled up her skirt to display her delightful nylon-clad leg and was adjusting her suspender. Miller didn't seem to notice. Niven did. His heart leapt and immediately he set about planning to date Heidi – if that was her real name – naturally, as he would explain later with a knowing wink, only in the line of duty.

'What I can't figure out, David,' Miller was saying while sipping his coffee with a grumpy look on his long, lantern-jawed face, 'is why Ike wants me to go to all this trouble to broadcast to a bunch o' Nazi Krauts. I mean, I came over here to entertain our own boys, not the Jerries.'

Niven fielded the complaint easily again. 'As I've already said, Glenn, ours is not to reason why. Anyway,' he added with apparent casualness, looking at the floor as if there were something very interesting going on there, 'you're invited to lunch after this business is finished. Not far from here, and they tell me they've got a damned good cellar ... air-raid *not* wine.' He laughed at his own joke. 'The White Tower in Henrietta Street.'

'Lunch? ... With who?'

'One of those hush-hush boys of yours,' Niven lowered his voice, as if the Germans might well be listening at the nearest door. 'He'll explain all, I'm told.'

'Explain all? ... hush-hush boys?' Miller stuttered, suddenly very much out of his depth. 'But what's all this got to do with me?'

Niven could have laughed at the other man's dismay. A little maliciously, he told himself that for the very first time Miller was being confronted by the harsh realities of World War Two. This was not the mock heroics of Hollywood, where the good guys always won, and after the final scene the dead rose once more and asked for a milk shake or a sandwich. Aloud he said, 'Search me, Glenn. I'm telling you just as much as I've been told.'

Miller opened his mouth as if to ask some more questions. But he didn't get a chance to do so. For the studio manager said, 'Major Miller, would you like to come over. We're ready for the next record now.' He spoke in an accent which Niven suddenly realised – with his acute ear for accents – was not totally English.

Dutifully, Miller, who was renowned for his own personal discipline and that which he imposed on his Air Force Band, responded immediately. He put down his mug and walked smartly across the darkened studio to where the fat little studio manager and the girl were waiting.

Niven noted that she had not only worked on her nylons, but also on her bust too. It looked bigger somehow. He grinned. It was the same old deal. How often had he seen it in Hollywood, which was full of rich, powerful old lechers who were not exactly the answer to a -maiden's prayer? Not that there were many maidens left in Tinseltown. Power, it seemed, was the ultimate aphrodisiac. He sighed. In such a world a forgotten movie star and lowly half-colonel like himself was not even in the running. He'd leave the delightful Heidi, or whatever she was called, to Glenn...

'All right, Major Miller,' she was saying, ' *"Fuenf"* please not *" funf"!'*

Niven grinned. Well, he'd have to pay for his supper at least. That is, if the good major knew he was being offered it...

# Two

'Incident, sir ... a bad 'un,' the middle-aged War Reserve constable in the battered tin hat said as he stopped their taxi and saluted when he saw the uniforms. 'Bus hit.' He spotted Heidi at the back, squashed in next to a hitherto happy David Niven, and added somberly, 'Wouldn't look if I was you, Miss ... Not a nice sight. All right, carry on, cabbie, and be sharpish about it. We're expecting the ambulances at any moment.'

The cabbie nodded. There was none of the customary flippant backchat between the cockney driver and the cop. The former could see that the 'incident' was very serious. The V-1 had come down right in front of the red double-decker. The driver had braked too late. He'd gone right into the crater and the sudden blast. There were dead bodies everywhere, some of them hanging from the lampposts like limp human fruit, dripping thick red juice.

'God almighty!' Glenn Miller gasped and held his hand to his thin-lipped mouth as if he might vomit at any moment. But the girl and the little studio manager – who was also cadging a lift with the two officers – were strangely unmoved, especially Heidi. Even the crazy woman with the dust-filled hair – suckling a dead baby at her full, blue-veined breast, crooning to herself as she did so – didn't seem to move the girl. She stared at the distraught mother as if she were a creature from another, alien world, which had nothing to do with her. Slowly the cabbie edged his ancient vehicle round the hole that almost filled Tottenham Court Road, while Miller continued to gasp and the other two remained obstinately silent and without reaction.

Once a nauseated Niven heard the taxi's wheels crunch over something soft and pulpy. He didn't dare look back and attempt to find out what it was. But he guessed the cabbie had driven over a body. Finally, they were through, and by now Niven was no longer interested even in pressing his thigh against the silk-clad one of his companion. All he wanted at that moment was to get away from this place, be sick and then sink a double whisky to clear his throat.

Opposite, the studio manager with the strange accent was saying to Miller, 'When and where do you think they'll use these German recordings, sir? Be interested in hearing the Krauts' reaction.' To which Miller answered truthfully, 'Hal, I don't have an idea in hell!'

Niven did. But at this moment he had no intention of saying; he was afraid that once he opened his mouth he'd spill his guts.

They turned left into Henrietta Street. Heidi's knee bumped against Niven's, accidentally or on purpose the one-time movie star didn't know or care. He felt the old thrill surging through his loins, and Miller, the strange recordings in German, and all the rest of what was proposed for that remote commercial radio station fled from his mind. Now his sole and major concern was to date the girl next to him. Casually, he dropped his suddenly sweating hand on her knee. She didn't flinch. He smiled to himself. The old phrase of those gay bachelor days in Hollywood flashed through his mind, *In like Flynn*. He was almost inside those pearly gates...

Miller felt a little uneasy. In his days in Hollywood and New York he had dined in many a swank restaurant. Hell, he had eaten in the Twenty-One Club nearly once a week in the old days. But this Greek restaurant in a shabby London side-street made him feel a little uneasy.

There were other Yanks in the place. But there was none of the glad-handing and table-hopping that he had been used to in Tinseltown. These Americans kept to themselves, engrossed as they all seemed to be in whispered conversation. And they were all sipping red wine, unlike the side-cars and Tom Collins he was used to. In short, he felt out of place, despite the fact that all of the Americans present were in military uniform, save one bearded giant who looked about sixty and was wearing a kind of uniform the like of which he had never seen before.

Abruptly, Miller felt very lonely and out of place and wished he was back in his familiar stamping grounds, back in the States. Niven should never have left him here like this to meet the unknown chap from intelligence by himself. Naturally, Niven had his eye on the blonde. The limey could never let up on the dames; it was a wonder he had any time to play soldier-boy.

The old man with the beard had raised his balding head from a deep conversation with a sharp-faced blonde who looked thirty years younger than he was, and now he struck his massive fist down on the table. The Greek owner, squatting behind the cash register near the door of the restaurant, looked up in alarm. Obviously, he was worried about his glasses, which Miller knew were in short supply, like everything else in this goddam island. Miller took a hesitant sip at the red wine they had brought him. He wrinkled his nose and wished he could have dared to order a beer.

But he guessed that in the White Tower they wouldn't even serve that weak, warm piss the limeys called beer.

Idly, Miller watched as the big, bearded man brought his fist down once again. Behind his till Mr Stais, the owner of the White Tower, held his hand to his head in the gesture of a sorely afflicted man. Miller wondered why the owner didn't interfere. Was the man, who was now going a puce colour with rage, some sort of VIP, as they were now calling big shots back in the States?

The woman, dressed in a smart pin-stripe suit which looked as if it had been cut down and tailored from a man's suit, took off her jacket. She was obviously hot and bothered by her drunken companion's behaviour. Miller gulped. The woman had a spectacular pair of tits, unfettered by any bra. Even at that distance and not possessing the best of eyesight, Miller could see the woman's big nipples protruding through the material of her sweater. Someone close to Miller's table gave a wolf-whistle, followed by a hot-breathed *hubba-hubba-hubba*, the way the GIs showed their appreciation of the female form.

The sound enraged the big man even more. He sprang to his feet, nearly over-turning the tight little restaurant table. The woman with the spectacular tits grabbed at his big paw and said something urgently. The big man flung her restraining hand to one side. His faded blue eyes glittered with rage. 'Who gave that wolf-whistle?' His voice was steady and educated but full of drunken menace. Suddenly his gaze fell on the lone Major Miller. 'Hey, you ... Major! Did you whistle?' he demanded, and clenched his big, gnarled fist.

Miller didn't know quite how to answer. He had grown up in the rough-and-tough atmosphere of clubs, where drunken brawls had been commonplace. But in these latter years, after the success of his two Hollywood movies, he had left that kind of life. Now even the minor gangsters and tough guys that you found in the top places showed him respect. After all, he was a 'name'. How did you cope with a big dangerous thug like this? He'd forgotten the drill. 'I ... didn't...' he stuttered.

The big guy was obviously not listening. He swaggered across the room and, towering above Miller, his fists clenched threateningly, he snarled, 'All right, smart ass, stand up and take your punishment like a man!' He stopped abruptly. 'I know you,' he said, tone softer now.

Miller breathed an inner sigh of relief. His unpleasant ordeal was over. But Miller was wrong. It had just started.

The big man peered closer at Miller, so

that the latter could smell his alcohol-laden breath, and said, 'Why, you're that faggot bandleader Glenn Miller, aren't you? Surprised you whistled. I thought all you guys were queer?'

Miller's pale face flushed. 'You have no right to talk to me like that...'

'I can talk any goddam way I like,' the other man cut him off smartly. 'My name's Hemingway. I'm a real artist, not a frigging fruitcake waving a wand in front of a bunch of drunks, turning our kids into softies. I don't hold any truck with perverters of youth like you, Miller.'

Miller tried to rise, muttering something about, 'I'm not sitting here to be insulted.' But Hemingway didn't let him. He pushed out a big paw. It struck Miller in the chest, knocking the breath out of him so that he gasped and sat down hastily like an abruptly deflated balloon. 'You sit down, Miller, till I tell you to get up, faggot!' Hemingway snarled, the bully in his personality taking over now. 'And when you do, I'm gonna knock the living shit outa...'

'Stop that at once, Mr Hemingway.' The voice was soft, but hard and incisive. It was the voice of someone used to giving orders; and having them obeyed.

For a moment or two Hemingway didn't seem to hear. Perhaps he was carried away by his drunken unreasoning rage; perhaps he wanted to impress the woman with the splendid tits; or perhaps he just wanted to work off steam and punch somebody. He drew his mighty paw back, preparatory to landing a haymaker on his unfortunate prisoner.

But that wasn't to be. Suddenly, startlingly, Hemingway had released his grip on Glenn Miller and was going down on his knees, and for the first time the bandleader caught a glimpse of his rescuer, a skinny little man with a wrinkled face, brown as a nut. Desperately, Hemingway tried to get up again. The little man kneed him in the back of his right knee once more. He slipped further. As he went down this time, the little man, without apparently making much of an effort, gave him a neat two-knuckled rabbit punch, and Hemingway pitched forward on to his face. He was probably unconscious before he hit the floor.

The little man pushed aside his plate of game – the waiter had been unable to tell them what kind it was, though the little man opined it was 'what the Italians call "roof hare", ie cat' – and said, 'I think that's enough for yours truly, Major Miller.' Miller nodded. That remark about roof hare had put him off for a start, and the soggy Brussels sprouts – which, he had often remarked, 'only the limeys can eat' – hadn't helped much. Now he looked forward to the only thing the English couldn't spoil: ice cream.

The little man with the nut-brown face and eyes that sparkled like black diamonds had decided he didn't want the 'pudding' the English seemed to call all desserts, and settled for a double scotch. Now, as the restaurant emptied and a sore, but pacified Hemingway staggered out – not venturing one glance in their direction, supported by the woman with the splendid tits – the little man, who had still not introduced himself – in the end he never would – said softly, 'Sorry for all this hush-hush stuff, Major. But I think you'll see that it is necessary, very necessary.'

Miller nodded as if he understood, although in reality he was completely confused. But still, it had been a funny day altogether, what with the doodlebugs and the drunken writer; a day when anything could happen and probably would. So he didn't comment.

The little man, who Miller had by now named Smith – that would probably be the name he'd use if he ever did give it – sipped his scotch thoughtfully, as if he were trying to work out how to start. Finally, he said, 'On the face of it, General Eisenhower wants you to broadcast from Radio Luxembourg in German in order to convince the Germans we're not all barbarians. If they defect and come over to us, they'll receive fair treatment. In particular, you and your music – *Schwingmusik*, as they call it – appeal to the younger generation, the front-line infantry; the ones we want to desert, for obvious reasons.'

Miller nodded carefully, but said nothing. Out of the corner of his eye, he could see the owner personally supervising the preparation of his ice cream, the manufacture of which, he knew, was forbidden in strictly rationed Britain. This was a black market item; his host would have had to pay through the nose for it.

'Over the next few weeks we hope to build you up as a focal point for the Germans, Major ... a kind of good humour man. Someone they can relate to.'

'Why?'

Smith didn't answer.

'Once that has been achieved we can expand your role ... *considerably*.' He emphasised the word for reasons known only to himself, but the emphasis made Miller feel uneasy for some reason he couldn't fathom. He said, 'What role ... and how is it to be expanded?'

But before 'Smith' could reply, the waiter appeared, soft-footed and beaming, to bow and present the ice-cream on a silver dish, 'Your ice cream, sir!'

'Smith' beamed too. To Miller's surprise,

103

he leaned forward and dipped his forefinger in the pink mix – dyed with the aid of beetroot – saying, 'You must eat it all up, Major ... Hm, does that taste good!' His smile increased even more and he added, 'Why that's the first ice cream I've tasted since 1942. Now come on, Glenn, eat up every last precious morsel.'

Obediently, Miller picked up his spoon and started eating the artificial mess. It was only later that he asked himself where Smith, an American like himself, could have been for the last two years and not tasted an ice cream?

# Three

Miller was worried, puzzled and not even quite sure where he was. The V-1 attack had seemingly swept the taxis from Central London's streets. Not even his American officer's uniform, usually a guarantee of a big tip, had convinced one of the few cabs he had spotted speeding down Tottenham Court Road to stop. As for Smith, he hadn't offered any help and he had disappeared from the White Tower almost as mysteriously as he had appeared to bring Hemingway down to his knees in both senses of the phrase.

Still, Miller was glad in one way of the respite from talk and explanations. The time out on the street did give him a chance to mull over what Smith had told him, or had been willing to tell him. The little man had confirmed what he had learned from that brief interview with his new fan, Ike, at the Hotel Alpha HQ in Luxembourg City. The recordings which the Supreme Commander had asked him to make and broadcast from that hickville radio station on the hill were of more importance than he had originally thought. They were not some crazy idea dreamed up by an obscure *psychwar* jerk. They were more, part of a much bigger plan that might influence the whole course of the war on the Western Front, according to Smith.

At that juncture he had asked Smith, baldly, 'How?'

And, as was seemingly customary with the little man with those sharp, dark eyes who hadn't eaten ice cream for two years, he had not answered directly. Instead, he had answered, 'Regard Radio Luxembourg as a message centre, Major Miller ... and, if we are lucky enough to strike gold, perhaps a place of meeting.'

Both terms, *message centre* and *place of meeting*, had puzzled him even more. But it had become clear to him that he was expected to go to Luxembourg personally when the first set of records with their German commentary was broadcast and then promise his unknown audience that he'd 'be around again' soon (those were Smith's exact words, *'and you must stick to them, Major'*). Thereafter, he was to play, as his penultimate record, a corny piece of schmalz by the English warbler, Vera Lynn, called 'I'll Be Seeing You'. Even as he walked down the deserted street, his face contorted with disgust at the thought of that horrible singer and her horrible piece of Yiddish crap.

He passed a bombed-out radio shop with the stark warning in its shattered front, *Looters Will Be Shot*. Below, some wag had cocked a snook at authority and had drawn the usual long-nosed figure peering over a brick wall with the legend: *Wot, No Free Gifts?* Miller sniffed. He had little sense of humour. Besides, he never understood what passed for a joke in England. Give him Hope and his wisecracks any day. He walked on, still obsessed by his problem.

Glenn Miller was a patriot, an American patriot. Back in 1942 he had volunteered for the Army, and then the Navy. Both had turned down the family man in his late thirties. Finally, the Army Air Corps had accepted him, not in a combat role, but as a bandleader (after all, he had worn glasses since his youth). At first it had been in military bands, but he had soon thrown Souza and all the rest of those old-time military composers overboard and transformed military music in a manner that had shocked many.

Although his new military swing, with the razzamatazz and named soloists, had kept his name before the public's eye in this time of total war, Miller the patriot still wanted to do his duty by his native land. Now he was being offered a chance to do something that was potentially dangerous. After all, Radio Luxembourg's broadcasting station was a mere ten miles from the fighting front. The Krauts could raid it easily, he figured. So, was he going to risk his life out there? Was his own future and that of his wife and family to be placed in danger just for the sake of a few swing records announced in German? He paused suddenly and considered. It was a big decision to make.

Opposite, a flapping news-vendor's poster proclaimed, *Yanks Fighting in Central Aachen ... Jerry city expected to fall soon!* Miller didn't know where Aachen was, and he didn't care. Suddenly, with a feeling of overwhelming sexual desire, he longed to be safely back home in the States, his only worry the next booking and how to rescore a piece of music for the old Glenn Miller Orchestra.

'Good news, Major Miller, eh?' The oddly familiar voice cut cheerfully into his worried reverie. He turned, startled.

It was the studio manager from the recording place, the one who had found the pretty German-speaking blonde, who Niven was now probably laying in his smart Chelsea flat.

'Yes,' the little civilian said, 'now those Jerries'll find out what it's like to have our lads fighting in their bloody cities. Serves 'em right, don't you agree, Major?'

'Yes, yes,' Miller agreed, confused even

more by his sudden and surprising appearance in this deserted street. 'I guess you're right.'

'You Yanks are really showing the Jerries what for. It won't be long now, Major,' he added cheerfully, 'and you'll all be able to go back home ... and I'm sure you'll be glad to do so!' He swept his pudgy hand across the shattered landscape. 'This ain't the best way to live, is it? Puts the mockers on yer, don't it?'

Miller nodded his agreement and then – suddenly glad of the company, even if it was only this small, insignificant limey, who'd pass out of his life totally once this afternoon came to an end – he ventured, 'What about walking back to the studio together? I left my horn there and most of my heavy gear.'

The other man actually blushed. 'Why, of course, Major! It'll be a pleasure. What a treat. Wait till I tell my missus that I went for a walk with Glenn Miller of Hollywood. She'll do her nut, God bless 'er. She's seen both your pictures, you know. She 'specially liked that bit in *Orchestra Wives*.' Chatting away as if they were the oldest of friends, he took Miller's arm and started to lead him back to the studio.

The tail watched them go down the street in the direction of the tube station at the corner and shook his head in mock wonder.

Then, as the sirens began to sound their dire warning once again, he broke into a run, heading for the nearest shelter as fast as his legs could take him. Up above, watching the whole business through his binoculars, the man Miller called Smith for want of a better name shook his head too. But it wasn't in wonder, it was a kind of self-congratulation. He lowered his glasses and the captain with the Sphinx badge of the US Counter-Intelligence Corps on the lapels of his 'Ike' jacket said, 'They've bought it, Jebb?'

The other nodded. 'Yeah,' he said laconically.

'So, Major Miller's a marked man from now onwards. Do you think they'll try something drast...'

'Don't even ask,' Smith, or Jebb – for neither was his true name – cut him short. 'This is going to be a very nasty game, Captain, a very nasty game indeed.'

'That's the name of our business, Jebb,' the young counter-intelligence officer said cheerfully enough. 'You know what they say ... you can't make an omelette without breaking eggs.'

Smith wasn't impressed by the glib expression. 'Maybe. But remember, in 1944 eggs to be broken are in very short supply. All right.' He was businesslike now. 'Let's get on the stick. Liaise with the British.

Their MI5 guys are all right, but keep MI6 out of it, if you can. Those upper-class gents of theirs would sell their own grandmas down the river for five bucks. Ensure Miller is under some sort of guard everywhere he goes from now on. I'll take care of the Luxembourg end. Hell,' Smith's face broke into a wintry, cynical grin, 'we can't afford to lose Mr Glenn Miller. I mean to say, Captain, what would the Great American Public do if we got the creator of that classic, "In the Mood", murdered, eh?'

The CIC captain didn't rise to the bait. Instead, he answered laconically, 'Wilco, Jebb.'

A minute or so later, the little man who Miller had named Smith had gone, covering his tracks by using the pavement closest to the captain's place of observation, so that he couldn't see which way he had taken. The latter sniffed and told himself that it was typical of the man. He was always on his guard, and he was the guy who mocked the British for selling their grandmas down the river for five bucks. Hell, Jebb would throw in his grandpa too for another buck!

# Bloody Aachen
# October 1944

# One

Aachen was dying.

Rapidly, inexorably, it was being eaten up by the greedy, clawing, red flames of the thousands of enemy incendiaries. Time and time again the Ami Thunderbolts came zooming in at roof-top height to drop their deadly loads with impunity. From the suburbs, now in US hands, their artillery thundered and added high explosive shells to the rapid destruction of the old German Imperial city. The GIs of the Big Red One, the US 1st Infantry Division, even packed the municipal trams with high explosive and sent them rattling down the hills to explode in the hollows below. On all sides there were flames, buildings were shaking and falling apart like stage backdrops and ruins were slithering down in an avalanche of bricks and masonry. It would be only a matter of days, perhaps hours now, before the whole city centre lay in ruins, and those who were trying so desperately to defend the city of the Holy Roman German Emperors became buried beneath the smoking debris.

What was left of SS Wotan had been thrown into the defence of the border city pretty late in the battle. Reichsführer SS Himmler had only agreed to use his premier SS regiment in this lost battle when the Führer himself had insisted. The SS had to be used to bolster up the battle commandant's weakening, ragtag defence force so that they fought to the bitter end. Aachen would 'never surrender,' the Führer had raged, frothing at the corners of his mouth, carried away by one of his unreasoning outbursts of temper.

But Obersturmbannführer von Dodenburg was determined that his beloved regiment would not be thrown away uselessly in some symbolic struggle that Germany could not win. There would be no second Stalingrad for Wotan. He would protect his brave young SS men and when he thought the time was ripe and Aachen was irretrievably lost, he would pull the survivors out to fight another day, whatever the Führer or Himmler said to the contrary.

Now he pulled his survivors back yet again, while the rearguard mortared the Amis, who were gathering for another attack out of the ruined, smoking houses to the left. In the lead personnel carrier, he could smell the sweet stench of death everywhere, even above the acrid smoke rising from the bank to his left, which was blazing fiercely.

Von Dodenburg shielded his eyes against the orange glare. Before him, the remaining houses wavered as if seen in some desert mirage. He squirmed round in the tight confines of the personnel carrier, its metal sides already beginning to glow in the reflected heat. 'Schulze,' he yelled above the thunder of the enemy artillery, 'we're going through! It's the only way. Tell the men to put on their gas-masks.'

Schulze opened his mouth to protest. The Amis had snipers everywhere on the roof-tops. The young grenadiers packed like sardines in the open personnel carriers were easy targets. But an impatient, red-faced von Dodenburg brooked no objections. 'Tell 'em!' he roared.

'All right,' Schulze ordered, 'you heard the officer. And you greenhorns, piss on yer snot rags and hold 'em over yer turnips!' He meant heads. 'Keep the flames from singe-ing yer grey matter. *Los!*' Without waiting to see if they carried out his command, he pulled out his gas-mask from its metal case, tugged it on and pulled out his penis.

'Need a hand to find it, Sarge?' Matz enquired, doing the same.

As tense as he was, von Dodenburg grin-ned. What a blessing these old hares were. They defused even the worst of situations. Then he forgot the two old rogues. He slam-med his hand down on the frightened young driver's shoulder and shouted above the roar of the guns and the obscene belch and thump of his own mortars. 'Roll 'em!'

The masked driver needed no urging. He thrust home first gear. The armoured personnel carrier creaked rustily and then started to move forward. Behind them the rest of the convoy followed. Almost immediately, the snipers waiting for them on the roofs opened fire. Here and there men shrieked with sudden pain. They clasped hands to shoulders and chests, and pitched forward on to their comrades packed in the open carriers. Next to Matz a young grenadier – he looked barely older than fourteen – screamed with agony. A bullet had gone right through the top of his right eye. Now it dangled down his ashen cheek like some hideous marble. Blood jetted in a scarlet arc from the abruptly empty eye socket.

'You bastards!' Matz yelled crazily. Standing upright, ignoring the slugs cutting the air all around him, he levelled his machine pistol. Without appearing to aim, he sprayed the roofs above the desperate little column. Remaining windows shattered. Masonry and timber splintered. Brick dust rained down in red fury. A sniper screamed shrilly. He dropped his telescopic rifle. Next instant he was sailing downwards in a crazy profusion of whirling limbs, dragging his last scream behind him. He hit the debris-littered cobbles below. He bounced once and fell again to the ground, every bone in his limp, crumpled body shattered.

The convoy pushed on. Destruction and flames engulfed them. The steel plates glowed a dull red. The grenadiers huddled together in terror. Even the snipers were forgotten. Twice they were stopped as enemy fighter bombers came zooming in, cannon flashing in a red-and-white fury. Bombs exploded almost immediately. The blast whipped their sickly-white, terrified faces. The very air was dragged out of their lungs, so that they coughed and choked like ancient asthmatics in the throes of a final, fatal attack.

And then they were through. They had broken out of the Ami trap and were back in their own perimeter, centred on the big bunker which was the headquarters of the Battle Commandant, Oberst Wilck. Von Dodenburg didn't hesitate. They had to get away from the vehicles. They'd come back for them later when the barrage had ceased, if they were still there and intact. *'Alle 'raus!'* he yelled above the ear-splitting noise of battle. *'Dalli ... dalli ... Raus!'*

The survivors needed no urging. Crouched low, they swung themselves over the glowing sides of the carriers and doubled for the nearest cover before the enemy single-winged spotter planes circling above like metal birds of prey radioed back their positions to the Ami artillery.

Outside, all was chaos. A group of panic-stricken German Army amputees in blue-and-white striped pyjamas and smocks burst out to meet them, hopping along on one leg or dragging those who had lost both legs. Some, like crazy midgets, propelled themselves forward on little homemade wooden carts. Von Dodenburg swallowed the sudden lump in his throat. What hell these poor cripples were going through, especially those who had lost a limb and had been blinded too! 'Help those men,' he yelled. 'Get them to shelter ... in God's name!'

A woman ran through the bunch of panzer grenadiers in their camouflaged overalls. She was screaming, blank-eyed and demented with terror. She had torn off her scorched blouse to reveal fat breasts, both burning with the white phosphorus that had buried itself in her naked flesh. 'Stop her!' von Dodenburg yelled urgently.

Schulze dived for the crazy woman, whose breasts were beginning to shrivel a crinkly, stinking black. He missed. Matz stuck out his peg-leg. She skipped over it and ran on, screaming all the time. She was heading for her doom, von Dodenburg knew. She needed water to cut off the air which kept the white phosphorous pellets embedded in her breasts burning. But there was no water. He took aim with his machine pistol. He pressed the trigger. It erupted into violent life at his hip. The woman flung up her arms, sudden bloody button-holes stitched the length of her naked white back. It was as if she were climbing the rungs of a ladder, perhaps to salvation and heaven. But there was no salvation or heaven in Aachen this October day. Next moment she slammed to the cobbles and writhed for a while as she continued to burn, filling the air suddenly with the cloying, sweet smell of roasted human flesh.

'*Mir nach!*' von Dodenburg yelled. He had to get his survivors under cover. For already they had been spotted by one of the damned little Ami spotter planes and he didn't need a crystal ball to know the pilot-observer was radioing their position to his battery. He darted forward. He skipped over barricades and piles of smoking rubble like a ballet-dancer. 'Come on,' Schulze shrieked behind him, 'haul ass, you bunch o' asparagus Tarzans!' Blindly, he fired a burst at the spotter plane.

They ran past a fire-engine. It looked in perfect order. Its engine was ticking over softly. There wasn't a mark on it. But the firemen perched on either side of the ladder had suffocated in the searing heat. They were all dead, their uniforms burned away without trace, naked save for their helmets and big, black boots.

Von Dodenburg felt the hot vomit surge up into his throat. He was going to be sick at the terrible sight. He caught himself just in time, and swallowed the bitter, green bile. He didn't have the time for personal indulgence. He had to save his men. He ran, desperately seeking cover for the survivors. Behind him, the petrol tank of the engine exploded. The naked bodies were flung into the skeletal trees on both sides of the road, where they hung disconcertingly.

They swung round a corner. Prisoners in striped, pyjama-like uniforms were mechanically pulling dead babies from the trees. They gaggled and giggled as they did so, mindless of the explosions all around them. Were they mad? Were they drunk? Von Dodenburg never found out. At that moment an Ami fighter came sweeping right down the centre of the street at roof-top height, machine guns blazing. Tracer scythed into the crazy prisoners and their burdens. They were wiped away as if by a big hand swatting flies. Abruptly, the gutters were full of dead babies and dying, screaming prisoners, twisting and writhing, choking on their own hot blood.

But slowly the noise of battle started to decrease. The Ami thrust for Aachen's command bunker had run out of steam. The fire slackened, and the observer planes began to depart for their bases, just over the border in Belgium and Holland, to refuel ready for the next attack. An exhausted von Dodenburg signalled his men to relax. Behind him Schulze, as bold and belligerent as ever, growled, 'All right, you bunch of piss pansies, broken step now ... march! Relax,' he grinned wickedly, 'we don't want yer getting yer monthlies just now.'

Von Dodenburg shook his head in mock wonder. Nothing, but nothing, seemed to be able to get Schulze and his running mate Matz down. In silence they marched on, grey-faced and hollow-cheeked, like a line of silent ghosts.

Now, through the drifting smoke and fog of war, they could see the big square bunker, its concrete sides scarred by shell-fire like the symptoms of some loathsome skin disease. This was Oberst Wilck's HQ and von Dodenburg was pleased to see it. For he was going to ask Wilck, an aged infantry commander, for something the latter wouldn't like: to ask Reichsführer SS Himmler for permission for them to break out. His excuse would be that there was no room for an armoured assault regiment in Aachen. This was hand-to-hand fighting. Armoured fighting vehicles were wasted in such places and, God knows, Germany needed all the armour it possessed.

They started to pass through a confused mass of civilians: old men, women and kids. They were fleeing the city again while the barrage had ceased. They had wet rags wrapped around their faces; with pans and first world war helmets on their heads. Anything to protect themselves. They stepped on the dead bodies which lay everywhere in the grotesque, extravagant postures of those done violently to death. Dogs scavenged, looking for meat, human or otherwise. No one cared. It seemed to be every man for himself, von Dodenburg told himself. It was time for Wotan to get out.

They had almost reached the command bunker now. But they were stopped momentarily by a chain-dog. The military policeman with the silver chain and gorget of his office around his neck said, 'Won't take half a mo, Obersturm.' He indicated the group of sweating, filthy engineers under the command of a young, arrogant-looking officer. 'They're gonna blow up that shelter to make a firebreak ... and a field of fire for the command bunker.' He gave a little sigh, and von Dodenburg told himself it was a bad sign; chain-dogs usually never showed any emotion but anger.

'But there's kids and women still inside!' a middle-aged woman with singed hair was crying. 'I heard 'em crying in there only a few minutes ago, Herr Leutnant.'

The arrogant-looking engineer ignored the hysterical woman. He got on with his task as if he were back in the depot practising some routine.

'If there was a God,' the middle-aged woman said sadly when she saw her words were having no effect, 'He wouldn't let this sort of piggery happen.'

An old man with a first world war moustache snapped, 'Leave Him out of this! God doesn't make war, woman. *Men* do!'

'But...'

The woman's objection was cut off by the roar of explosives as the young officer pressed the detonator plunger. The top of the building collapsed neatly in an avalanche of falling bricks and stones. They buried the air shelter below. If there were kids and women still in there, they'd die a lingering death as their oxygen gave out.

It was all clinical and clean. The engineers picked up their equipment and wandered off to other jobs. The old man with the old-fashioned Kaiser Wilhelm moustache clicked to attention and saluted the shattered building for some reason known only to himself; while the woman with the burned hair who had protested picked a can of food from the rubble, spat on the label to check what it contained, seemed pleased when she discovered what it was, and then hurried away, the can clutched to her hanging breasts.

Behind von Dodenburg, Schulze – not an emotional man by any means – muttered to himself, 'What a frigging life!' He sighed. 'Roll on death and let's have a go at the frigging angels!'

Von Dodenburg nodded, as if he agreed with the sentiment. He gave the signal to move on. To the west, the first of the refuel-led Ami spotter planes were ascending into the October sky. It was time to get Wotan under cover. A few minutes later, they were filing – suddenly weary, as if someone had opened a tap and allowed all energy to drain from their emaciated bodies – into the shelter of the great command bunker.

# Two

Oberst Wilck offered von Dodenburg a small cognac, measuring the spirits out carefully, as if it were very precious. He was weary and old-looking. Von Dodenburg guessed he was a 'retread': an officer brought out of retirement to make up for the tremendous loss in infantry officers in the last few years. He didn't show it too much, but it seemed to von Dodenburg that Wilck was out of his depth and at the end of his tether. Still, the man was bravely attempting to carry out his dangerous duty when he should be spending a slippered retirement tending his roses and sitting in front of the stove in the evenings, smoking his pipe peacefully and reading his Goethe.

'*Prosit, Herr Oberst!*' he toasted his superior, raising the little glass level with the third button of his tunic, arm set at a rigid forty-five degree angle as military protocol demanded.

'*Prosit, mein Lieber!*' Wilck answered, like some benevolent uncle with a favourite nephew. 'Thank you!' He drained his glass in one, as was required, and coughed.

'I don't know what I would have done without your assistance. My chaps are a mixed bunch, unfortunately.' He sighed like a sorely tried man. 'The High Command expects too much of them. Without your Wotan, I don't know what we would have done.' He shook his grey head.

Again von Dodenburg told himself that Aachen should have been evacuated weeks ago, as soon as the Americans had attacked. Its defence served no purpose; the main thing was to halt the Amis at the old city's double ring of Siegfried Line defences. But the Party was naturally concerned, as always, with prestige objectives, not sound military principles. He remarked aloud, as the muted rumble indicated that the enemy was attacking yet again, 'We did our best, Oberst.'

'More than your best. I hate to see young men's lives wasted...' He stopped short and looked anxiously at the SS officer, and the latter knew why. It had abruptly occurred to him that von Dodenburg of the Armoured SS was potentially an enemy. Ever since the Army had attempted to assassinate the Führer back in July, any and every Wehrmacht officer was suspect. At the slightest sign of defeatism, an army officer – whatever his rank – could be arrested. 'I have a signal for you from SS HQ,' Wilck said, recovering hastily, 'I think it might be important.'

Von Dodenburg rose and said, 'Thank you, Colonel. I have to go anyway and see how my rogues are being accommodated and fed. And, Colonel Wilck,' he hesitated too, for how did he know whether Wilck might betray him as well? 'Don't worry. You have my every respect, and I am sure the respect of the High Command and Party too.'

That made Wilck happy. He pulled out the radio signal and handed it to von Dodenburg. 'A bit strange in light of the situation here. But no matter ... and thank you, Obersturm ... I appreciate your confidence in me and my command...'

Five minutes later, von Dodenburg was sitting in the straw on the floor of the NCO's quarters in the bunker, back against the damp dripping concrete wall, perusing the signal which purported to come from Himmler's new SS HQ at Hohenlynchen near Berlin. But didn't. For the pencilled initials in the bottom box, *OS*, told him something different. As such, however, the radio message was innocuous; there had been no attempt even to put it into code. It was a clear, routine, low-grade communication which the Amis could read if they cared to.

While opposite him Sergeant Schulze

prized a couple of weeks' dirt out from beneath his brown toenails with the aid of his bayonet point, von Dodenburg studied the supposedly routine signal. It read:

In light of your brave and skilful efforts at the front, I wish you to stand the Regiment down for the next twenty-four hours. Double rations, plus a quarter of a litre of schnaps – or a bottle of beer – will be issued to each trooper over the age of 18. This order is to take effect immediately upon receipt.
Heil Hitler!
Reichsführer SS Himmler

Von Dodenburg looked thoughtful.

Opposite, Matz was moaning, 'For Chrissake, Schulze, put them frigging feet away again in yer dice-beaker!' He meant the big sergeant's jackboots. 'You'll frigging kill the lot of us with that pong!' To which Schulze replied calmly, 'Your farts don't exactly smell o' attar of roses, either, comrade!'

The business about no alcohol for any panzer grenadier under the age of 18 was typical of that bureaucratic prude Himmler, but the scribbled initials *OS* indicated that the message had not come from the most feared man in Europe. For Otto Skorzeny was the originator of the seemingly innocuous order. Ever since that ambush back in

September, he had been placed secretly under the command of Skorzeny's mysterious Jagdkommando. This signal had been arranged by Skorzeny before SS Assault Regiment Wotan had been transferred so suddenly from the SS Reserve Army to the fighting front in Aachen. It meant, in essence, that he was to report with his Regiment to Skorzeny within the next twenty-four hours. He wondered why. He frowned and told himself it was going to be a tall order.

Opposite, Schulze paused in what he called grandly, *my personal ablutions*, and seeing the look on von Dodenburg's harshly handsome face asked, 'Where's the fire, sir?'

By way of an answer, von Dodenburg beckoned him across and – taking the bayonet very gingerly from Schulze's big paw and wondering how great was the range of loathsome diseases he might catch from it – said softly, 'Keep it to yourself, you big rogue, but we're going to break out.'

'Well, I'll be rogered right royally in the rectum,' Schulze exclaimed.

Von Dodenburg might have laughed at the remark under other circumstances, but not now. For he knew any break-out from Aachen at the moment would be damned dangerous. Now he drew a circle in the concrete dust of the floor with Schulze's bayonet. He made a cross. 'Command bunker ...

131

with roads leading out to Cologne, Jülich, Maastricht. Naturally, all these main highways have been taken by the Amis or are under interdiction fire. They know that if any attempt at a break-out is made it will be in the direction of our lines to east or north.'

Schulze nodded his understanding. 'So, Wotan's going to break out, sir?'

'Keep it to a dull roar, Schulze. We must keep this as secret as possible. I wouldn't put it past the Amis to have spies in the city. Yes, the short answer is, we're breaking out in the next twenty-four hours.'

'How?' Now Schulze wasn't wasting any words.

'The way that'll give the Amis a surprise and might give us a head start before they tumble to what we're about. Through their lines to the west, along the frontier and back into our own lines in the Monschau area. Chancey, I know, but when has Wotan ever had it easy?' he laughed.

Schulze, for once, didn't respond. 'Risky, sir,' he said, with unusual caution for him. 'Very risky. But it's better,' his voice rose when he saw the look on von Dodenburg's lean face, 'than croaking it in this hole. As they say, the enemy's got us in the pisspot and now he's gonna piss on us!'

'Exactly, you big rogue!' von Dodenburg responded eagerly, glad of the old hare's sudden support.

'But sir,' Schulze said as an afterthought, 'what about these here hairy-assed stubble-hoppers?' he indicated with a jerk of his head the worn-out field greys lying listlessly in the lice-infested straw at the other side of the room. 'They ain't gonna like it one bit if we fart off without saying good-bye.'

Von Dodenburg nodded. 'Exactly. I don't like it either. It's a bit like rats abandoning the sinking ship. Still, it's an order, and my main aim in this war now is to save what I can of Wotan. That's all that counts.'

'Well said, sir,' Schulze agreed heartily. 'I'm sure even them Christmas-tree squaddies we have in Wotan these days would say yer right there, sir. But Colonel Wilck might try to stop us.'

'No one – in particular Colonel Wilck – is to know,' von Dodenburg urged in a warning voice. 'The men can be told they're to stand down, that's all. Let them have whatever high jinks this place offers till midnight.'

'I'll give 'em all a bag of boiled sweets and a dirty book and tell 'em they can have a crafty wank,' Schulze suggested with a coarse guffaw.

Von Dodenburg was forced to smile, despite his inner tension. Schulze was irrepressible. 'Anything you like, you dirty-mouthed devil, Schulze. But pass the word

133

to the old heads and NCOs that we move out at midnight.'

'Vehicles, sir?'

'We leave our armour and soft-skinned vehicles. We camouflage the personnel carriers. With a bit of luck the Amis might take them for their own half-tracks if they spot them.'

'They'd need their frigging glassy orbs testing if they *did*!' Schulze countered.

'Don't be a little ray of sunshine, Schulze,' von Dodenburg snapped. 'All right, you're on your own. Tell the men they're off duty till midnight.'

Schulze rose hastily and beamed down at the CO. 'Wine, women and song from here on in, sir, eh?'

'Something like that,' von Dodenburg answered and smiled. 'The men deserve whatever they get, you know, Schulze. They've done us proud.'

'Yessir,' Schulze replied dutifully, 'as long as they don't get a dose of clap!' He saluted, leaving von Dodenburg alone with his thoughts, which were not too happy. For he knew that the gap around Aachen was soon to be closed by the besieging Amis. It was a matter of a mere five hundred metres, and if the enemy were prepared to suffer a couple of hundred casualties to bridge that distance, then the old Imperial city would be totally surrounded, cut off from the rest of the Reich.

Oberst Wilck's adjutant had informed him that the Battle Commandant already had his last radio signal prepared for dispatch. It would read something like, 'All ammo gone ... no water or food. Enemy close to defenders of the command post. Radio prepared for destruction.' In other words, a dispirited, exhausted Wilck of the 246th People's Grenadier Division was about to give up. He and his Wotan, however, could have put enough backbone in to the defenders to keep the fight for the old Imperial city going for a little longer. So why would Skorzeny – acting with the possible approval of Reichsführer SS Himmler – have his regiment pulled out at this crucial moment? What was so important about whatever role Skorzeny – a man he didn't quite trust – had in mind for him? Von Dodenburg closed his eyes as if he wanted to blot out his surroundings and concentrate, or perhaps even drift into the blessed oblivion of sleep. But that wasn't to be. His mind kept working. In the end, he gave up. He placed his helmet on his head and tightened his pistol belt. There was only one thing for it. *A whore!*

# Three

Twenty miles away from that bunker, in the Belgian border town of Verviers, the Allied top brass were already celebrating the fall of Aachen. That Friday, in the centre of a muddy field, an army of GIs had erected a tented camp, filled in all the ruts and puddles made by their trucks, and systematically laid paths flanked by white posts and chains, and had even attempted to plant flowering shrubs brought in specially from nearby Maastricht; they hadn't lasted more than a couple of hours in the cold air. But after inspection by a two-star general and a host of engineers, sanitation experts, even senior cooks, the place was judged ready to receive the illustrious guests from Paris and London. Thereupon, the camp was surrounded by a belt of anti-aircraft guns, the tanks rolled up – two companies in brand new Shermans straight from the depot – and a whole battalion of the Big Red One took up their positions in the foxholes and gunpits dug for the infantry by the departing engineers. Finally, two bright new flags, those of Britain and America, were run up the flagpoles. General Eisenhower, the Supreme Commander, was ready to receive his guest, the master of one third of the whole world, the King Emperor himself, King George VI.

For both of them it had been a busy day. Eisenhower had made a brief appearance on the Aachen front. He had slipped in the thick, slick mud to the delight and cheers of his GIs. The King, for his part, had spent much more time at the Master's caravan and had drunk several cups of horrible compo ration tea, while the Master – Field Marshal Montgomery – had regaled him with boring stories from the front.

All had passed off smoothly, save that after a couple of hours travelling down the rutted, shell-pitted country roads of the front, US General Hart – in charge of the King's protective convoy – had been forced to stop the vehicles for some mysterious reason of his own.

A puzzled King George had summoned the General and stuttered, 'W ... w ... what was the pr ... problem, General Hart?'

A red-faced Hart had replied that he had been instrumental in stopping the vehicles because, 'I needed a comfort stop, sir.'

The King had been too shy to ask what a 'comfort stop' was; he had feared it might be some sort of esoteric American ritual, perhaps even sexual, about which it was better not to ask.

Now, however, the King was in high spirits, even his terrible stutter had, it seemed, diminished somewhat as the drink flowed and the American generals tried to outdo each other with their tales to impress George VI.

As usual, Eisenhower told himself, Georgie Patton tried to hog the show. He was the born exhibitionist. He related his adventures during the African campaign of the previous year at great length, remarking that even Allied wounded were not safe from the long fingers of the local Arabs, who stole everything that wasn't nailed down. He added, speaking directly to an intrigued King, 'Why, I must have shot a dozen Arabs myself, sir!'

Eisenhower looked at Patton and winked at a long-faced Bradley, who never seemed to enjoy anything, including good food and wine. 'How many did you say, George?' he asked.

'Well, maybe it was only half a dozen,' Patton conceded.

'*How many?*' Eisenhower persisted.

Patton looked directly at the monarch, 'Well, at any rate, sir,' he gave in, 'I did boot two of them squarely in the ... ah, *street* at Gafsa.'

The King giggled, holding his hand in

front of his mouth for some reason, as if he had bad teeth. It was the signal the generals were waiting for. They commenced laughing, too, even Eisenhower, though he wasn't in the best of moods. General Patton beamed. He loved it when he was the centre of attention as he was now. He had been in the dog-house so many times over these last months since he had entered battle again, it was great to be liked once more.

So they drank and gossiped and told their hoary old tales, while the British King giggled and stuttered and now and then looked suitably outraged, shocked, surprised, amused as the moment demanded. But Eisenhower for his part, although he kept that famous ear-to-ear smile on his broad face, felt his mind wandering.

Aachen would fall, he knew that. But he knew what it had cost the American Army in the way of bodies: nearly three thousand of them. If that was going to be the cost of every major town that the Army attacked, America would be fighting in goddam Germany for ever. Now, once Aachen was dealt with, it would be Patton's turn to take the fortified French frontier city of Metz, which he had boasted in early September he'd go through 'like shit through a goose'. Well, Georgie Patton had tried once and had failed: the damned goose must have been constipated! Now he'd turn on the works, and that would mean more dead riflemen; the bodies that were so vital to winning the war were mounting up at an alarming rate. He sighed.

In that same moment, tall, chinless Major General Strong – his Scottish chief-of-intelligence – came into the dining-room and headed straight for his commander-in-chief, walking almost silently, as if he didn't want the others – even his own king – to be aware of his presence. He bent over Ike's shoulder, hand held to the side of his mouth. 'Sir,' he whispered in that throaty Scots fashion of his which Eisenhower mostly found intriguing, though not now. He was too depressed by the way things were turning out on the Eifel-Ardennes front.

'What is it, Ken?' Eisenhower whispered back.

'It's on, sir. Just heard from London. From our man there. Miller's agreed.'

For a minute Eisenhower didn't seem to be able to take in the import of the message; perhaps he had drunk too much champagne with the King's lunch and everything, 'Operation...?'

'Yessir. Miller's agreed to go ahead with Operation Double Cross.' He pronounced the name of the operation as if the words themselves were lethal.

Ike's face lit up instantly for the first time

in many days. 'Holy mackerel. We're in business, Ken!'

The dark-faced Scot remained his usual sombre self. He had been in the nasty business of war – and, in particular, the very devious one of Intelligence – much longer than Ike. He was careful with his enthusiasm. 'We mustn't count the proverbial chickens before ... you know, sir.'

'Oh, come off it, Ken. This is a breakthrough. While we're feeding our faces here, our men are still dying by the score at the front. If we can pull this off it'll be all over and that terrible killing will cease.'

'Of course, sir,' Strong – the perfect senior staff officer – agreed immediately. 'But we, that is we British, have had dealings with the so-called German resistance,' he emphasised the word as if it were very distasteful to him, 'and nothing has ever come of it, save unpleasantness. One wonders what good will come of it now. Remember, sir – if I may add a warning – the German generals only tried to do away with their damned Führer when they realised they were losing the war ... and even then, with the whole of the Wehrmacht behind them, they made a hash of it. Now these survivors after the terrible German blood-letting of last July ... I mean,' Strong shrugged a little helplessly, 'are they capable of pulling it off this time, I ask you, sir?'

Eisenhower didn't even attempt to answer that overwhelming question. Instead, he said a little helplessly, 'All I know, Ken, is that we ought to at least try. We've got to end this bloody slaughter in the west soon ... or else.'

Ken Strong was a shrewd man. He didn't say it aloud, of course; but to himself he whispered, 'You're out of a job then, Ike, and your chances of ever becoming the president of the United States one day like General Grant will be virtually nil, old boy!' The tall, dark-faced Scottish general with the receding chin contented himself with, 'Is that all, sir? I'd like to get on with this thing.'

Eisenhower waved his hand in a kind of dismissal and said, ''Kay, Ken, get to it if you wish.'

As silently as he had appeared, he vanished, leaving Eisenhower listening to Patton, who was still hogging the conversation with King George VI. Flushed with drink and high spirits, Patton was saying, 'So, I tell my troops, your Majesty, that any soldier who won't fu ... excuse my French, sir ... fornicate won't fight.'

The poor, weak monarch who ruled a third of the world tittered, highly amused, and repeated the phrase with that awful stutter of his, 'I s ... say, that's rich ... The soldier who w ... won't f ... f ... fornicate won't f ... fight, ha ha!'

Patton was pleased. He hated the British like poison, yet it gave him the greatest of pleasure to be able to get their King to laugh. Eisenhower, watching in silence, worried beyond all measure and completely detached from the proceedings, wondered yet again how his generals, with the lives of thousands of young American soldiers in their hands, could be so happy.

Meanwhile, on the other side of the Channel, Major Glenn Miller packed his flight bag at the band's HQ in Bedford. He'd fly out by shuttle the following morning from the VIP air base at Bovingdon in the south. He too wasn't happy about what was to come. Patriot though he was, he had not bargained for this role, which smacked of espionage, and might even be dangerous too. Besides, he had to consider his wife Helen and the kids back in the States. Since he had volunteered for the Army his income had diminished and they were building that damned great house. If anything happened to him, all his widow would receive from a grateful United States of America was ten thousand dollars GI insurance. He couldn't afford to die just yet.

Miller paused in the midst of his packing. Somewhere in their billets one of the guys was practising his horn. He was doing well, and with a kind of everwhelming nostalgia he remembered how he had once been able to hit the notes sure, true and steady like that. But that seemed long ago now. Now he was an admin man, about to embark on a dangerous mission for his country. God, how he wished he could pack it all in and go back to what he had once been! But that wasn't to be. The States was bigger than all the Glenn Millers and their bands bundled together. He had to do his duty whether he liked it or not.

He finished his bag. Idly, he wandered down the hall into the fresh air. Some of the band were squatting on their cots playing poker. 'Do you want to sit in, Major?' one of them asked, twisting his unlit cigar stump from one side of his mobile mouth to the other.

'No thanks, Buddy!'

He moved forward again. Poker was another element from the past. He was an officer, a major now. He didn't play cards. He wasn't one of the boys. *But what am I?* he asked himself. *Where am I going, for God's sake?*

Above, a sudden cloud swept over the thin winter sun and blocked it out. A dark shadow fell across his homely face. Watching him, the little man who had been ordered to check the American's time of departure told himself that his target looked like a dead man already.

# Four

Sergeant Schulze raised his right haunch, stood thus while he emptied a flatman down his throat, his Adam's Apple racing up and down like an express lift, belched, wiped his dirty paw across his mouth and then broke wind with the impact of a 155mm howitzer being fired in a confined space. 'Holy straw-sack!' he exclaimed to no one in particular. 'I've got so much ink in me fountain pen, I don't frigging know who to write to first!' He stamped his heavily nailed jackboot down hard, as if to signify the ritual was at an end.

Next to him, Matz, who was making similar preparations for the night's sexual foray – it included some careful dusting of his sexual organ, or love tool, with a scented talcum powder – sneered, 'Do you think you'll make it? I mean, a woman like that with all that wood before the door ... and that scraggy little thing you've got dangling from between yer legs, Schulzi...'

Sergeant Schulze was too happy to be offended. 'Never you mind about me,

*Corporal* Matz. Once I get my head between those milk factories of hers and give 'em a wobble, I'll have no problem. Besides, she loves me.'

Ignoring Matz's hollow laughter at the statement, he crept out of the hole they shared and, crouching low, one hand holding his machine pistol, the other a bunch of dusty artificial flowers stolen from one of the shattered houses nearby, Sergeant Schulze set off for his 'rendezvous with me fiancée'.

Despite the nearness of the Amis, the constant artillery fire and the fact that she too was trapped, just like the soldiers, by the Ami encirclement, Frau Glücklich lived up to her name. Enormously fat, with a tremendous bosom the same size almost as the balcony of her shattered flat, she was frying potatoes over a makeshift stove in the flickering light of a couple of candles. 'Won't be long, my beloved big hero,' she chirped happily, the sweat dripping from her broad, red face. She bent and threw another piece of shattered timber on the fire. The movement caused one of her massive breasts to fall out of her low-cut peasant blouse. Routinely, she stuffed it back and Schulze chortled, 'Careful, my beloved. Fried tatties are enough. Don't want any meat!'

She laughed and wiggled her mighty

behind provocatively, 'Sergeant, Sergeant,' she exclaimed, 'you are a one! I never know what you'll get up to next.'

Schulze, eyeing those twin mountains of flesh, licked suddenly dry lips and answered, a little hoarsely this time, 'I'll give you one guess, my little cheetah.' He gave her bottom a playful slap which nearly sent her into the fire.

In another part of the cellars beneath Frau Glücklich's house, Matz too was enjoying his time out of the war. Unfortunately, he was still sober, unlike his running mate, Schulze. It was not a state to which he took kindly, especially when, as he put it with his usual sense of delicacy, 'a poor old stubble-hopper wants to get rid of his heavy water. It ain't natural. You've got to 'ave a dose o' the firewater to get the old mechanism started.'

It was for that reason that he and Heidi, Frau Glücklich's comely 15 year-old maid, had begun wandering down the dark cellars in search of firewater, only to chance upon a crimson-faced Senior Sergeant Schulze in one of his amorous moments. As was to be expected, he was naked save for his jackboots, pistol belt and helmet: 'A good soldier's allus prepared for anything, comrades!' In his left hand he had a half-emptied frying pan of potatoes, and with his other he held what appeared to Heidi at first sight to be a large policeman's truncheon. She soon decided it was something else and giggled dutifully behind her suddenly upraised palm as if the sight was just too much for her innocent – well, relatively innocent – gaze.

Hastily, Matz nudged her in the ribs, 'Don't disturb him on the frigging job,' he hissed warningly, 'there'll be all hell to pay. Besides, he's left his frigging flatman behind on that chair. Poor old shitheel. He must be *desperate for* it!'

And at that moment in time it seemed that Corporal Matz might well be right. For, cross-eyed with drink, Senior Sergeant Schulze was having some difficulty in carrying out his evil purpose with an eagerly squatting Frau Glücklich, her enormous naked rump raised for action.

'Looks as if he's having some trouble getting ready to fire his broadside at her,' Matz commented maliciously, as Schulze failed again and winced as if he had hurt himself.

'Why does he keeps banging that ... er ... thing of his against Madam's bottom?' Heidi enquired.

'Daft as a brush where he comes from,' Matz said. 'Couldn't get fucked in a knocking shop, even if they had a fifty mark note in their hands! Now shut up. I'm gonna get that flatman.' He licked his lips in anticipation. 'Heaven, arse and cloudburst, ain't my tonsils in for a frigging surprise!' He moved forward with astonishingly little noise for a man with a wooden leg. Heidi for her part tensed and watched open-eyed with awe as Schulze fumbled with that mighty truncheon and prepared to launch another broadside. 'Poor Madam,' she said, and uttered a quick prayer for her mistress and the rest of suffering womanhood.

Von Dodenburg staggered blindly through the smoking, burning streets of what was left of German-occupied Aachen. Despite the fresh Ami bombardment and their orders for later, there were similarly drunken Wotan troopers everywhere. Von Dodenburg didn't care. His mind's eye was still full of dead babies from the maternity hospital he had just passed, smoking and shattered.

It was the end. The end of everything. The world couldn't get worse. What did it matter if at midnight Wotan – what was left of it – got away or not? The world was crazy. The world was bad, unbelievably bad. What right had human beings to live, who did such things?

Another great 155mm howitzer shell exploded in the next street. Nearly, the walls of the ruined houses shimmied and trembled like a theatre backdrop caught by a sudden wind. Bricks and masonry slithered down in a red avalanche. Women screamed. Someone yelled in sudden agony, *'Sanitäter*

... *Sanitäter* ... my leg's off ... Stretcher-bearer, *please*!'

Von Dodenburg didn't seem even to hear. He blundered on, clambering over the smoking rubble, eyes intent on some far distant horizon known only to himself.

A couple of chain-dogs attempted to stop him, yelling above the screams and cries for help, 'Not that way, Obersturm ... It's too dangerous. There's an unexploded bomb...'

The words died on their lips. Obersturmbannführer von Dodenburg wasn't listening. They let him go and when he was out of earshot, one of them whispered to his fellow military policeman, 'Arrogant arseholes, these SS officers ... Hope the shitty bomb goes off right under him!'

But von Dodenburg was not fated to die just yet. Wotan wouldn't let him.

The whore put her firm arms around his neck and thrust her tongue between his lips. He stank of schnaps. But she didn't seem to care. In the haze that had settled around his crazy head now, he could see vaguely that she appeared to be very young for a professional whore, especially in strictly Catholic Aachen. And for some reason he couldn't fathom she was dressed in the white blouse and dark skirt of the League of German Maidens.

Also unlike the usual whore, the woman's whole body seemed to be trembling with desire. She kept thrusting her stomach into his and her hands were claws, scratching his back, as he tried to open his breeches. In the end she did it for him and – with hardly a word, her eyes fixed hypnotically on the opening in the breeches and what lay there – she fell back on the battered couch, slim legs spread, ripping at the buttons of her blouse.

It opened and her breasts fell out. They were large for her age, it seemed to his blurred gaze as he stood there swaying unsteadily.

She tugged off her knickers, white, simple and of cotton, the kind schoolgirls wore. Almost unconsciously, or so it appeared, she ran her hands over her naked breasts. Gently, she squeezed the pink nipples. They grew erect. Her ribcage heaved as if she had been suddenly seized by an almost uncontrollable passion. 'Come on,' she said, her voice hoarse and unsteady, 'please ... please ... do it!' She thrust up the thatch that decorated her white loins provocatively. 'Please Obersturmbannführer von Dodenburg!' She frowned heavily, as if she could hardly bear the tense waiting. 'Please.'

Von Dodenburg was instantly sober. Perhaps it was the fact that the supposed whore knew his name, or that he had abruptly realised she was wearing the uniform of the Hitler Maidens, and therefore had to be eighteen or under. 'But...' he stuttered, 'you are still in your teens.'

She laughed hollowly and opened her legs even wider. 'What difference does it make, Obersturm? You know we're all going to die. Sixteen or sixty,' she shrugged and her large breasts trembled delightfully. 'We're all the same ... perhaps a bit tighter, that's all.'

She raised her hands and thrust them into the dark cavern of his field-grey breeches. She cradled his penis like a fond mother might do a beloved child.

He shivered. Abruptly, the dam burst. He knew it was wrong, but he couldn't help it. He felt himself growing under her cunning little fingers. 'No...' he began. But he was unable to object any further. She drew him wordlessly down on to the couch. Greedily, she manipulated him. He was seized by an uncontrollable passion. 'Are you a virgin?' he asked thickly in a voice that he hardly recognised as his own. 'It'll hurt ... like this.'

She laughed, still holding on to him. 'Not any longer, my good sir.'

'But...'

'Shut up and enjoy!'

She raised her slim girl's legs into the air. They made a cradle for his hard, muscular body. 'I think it's time to climb aboard,' she whispered into his right ear. Her breath felt very hot. Greedily, she guided him to the entrance, her heart beating furiously.

For one last moment von Dodenburg hesitated. It wasn't right, he knew. Then lust and passion consumed him and he forgot his hesitations. He thrust himself into her cruelly. She gasped with pleasure, crying, 'Oh, my God!' Then both forgot anything and everything else. They surrendered themselves to love of a kind, while all around them their world went to pieces.

They were drinking from the bottle she had brought with her when she had first gone looking for him. 'I knew you were here, Obersturm. Before it all ended, I wanted to know what a hero was like...' She had broken off and he had laughed and snapped, 'God, I'm no hero, girl! I'm just a damfool stubble-hopper who's gonna get his stupid head blown off soon.' Then that familiar raucous Hamburg voice yelled from outside the ruin, 'Come on out, sir ... The war's over!'

Von Dodenburg groaned. It was Schulze. There was no mistaking those thick, beery tones. He put on his helmet first, out of a long-standing habit from the years of war in Russia. She gripped his hand tightly. 'Must you?'

He nodded and started doing up his flies.

Miserably, she put on her blouse and hid those beautiful young breasts of hers. 'I...'

He held his hand to her mouth gently and stifled her objection. 'No use,' he said

153

simply. 'No use whatsoever.'

Outside, Schulze and Matz and a young trooper were waiting for him, their faces blood-red in the fresh flames near Wilck's bunker. Von Dodenburg nodded. He understood without being told how Schulze and Matz had found him. They'd put the greenhorn on to tailing him. 'Well,' he snapped, slinging the machine pistol they had brought over his shoulder, 'where's the fire, you two rogues? It isn't midnight yet.'

'The field-greys are getting jumpy, sir,' Matz replied after taking another, last, crafty slug of Schulze's stolen flatman. 'Thought we'd better clear out before they start creaming their drawers. You know what those Christmas tree soldiers of the Army are like.'

Von Dodenburg nodded. 'All right, Schulze,' he said, turning to a somewhat sulky Sergeant Schulze, who for some reason was wearing a pair of large, red, artificial silk knickers draped around his helmet like some kind of bizarre camouflage. 'Where's the half-track?'

By way of an answer, Schulze turned to the greenhorn who had been the CO's tail and ordered, 'All right, sonny, go and start up the CO's vehicle. Daddy'll give you a sweetie if you're a good boy.'

The boy was about to say something, but then he saw the look on Sergeant Schulze's face and decided against it. He turned and doubled away as the barrage started to increase once more and Ami mortar bombs came whining down some fifty metres away.

'Now God's shitting steel on top of us,' Schulze said mournfully, totally unaware, it seemed, of the terrible blasphemy. 'Ain't there never gonna be a bit o' peace for yer poor old common-or-garden squaddie?'

Von Dodenburg thought of assuring him that there never would be, save beneath the ground, but thought better of it. Instead, he cried almost joyously, 'All right you two asparagus Tarzans, full o' piss and fried potatoes. *Los* ... let's move it!'

They moved it.

A few moments later the first half-track started to rattle by the lone girl crouched sobbing in the shadow of a ruined doorway. They were heading for the escape route and the fight to come. SS Assault Regiment Wotan was moving towards its new battle. Behind it, the old Imperial city of Aachen began to sink into the greedy flames.

# Book Two
# The Denouement

*'Mitgegangen, mitgefangen, mitgehangen .'*
*German Proverb*

# Ten Prinz Albrechtstrasse
# November 1944

# One

'So, the Yid bastard's here?' Obergruppenführer Müller said, looking up from his big
desk. Behind him, Berlin was quiet again
after the usual Tommy raid. The fire-engines
were departing to be replaced by what the
locals called *the grave robbers*: the usual
bunch of concentration camp prisoners in
their striped, pyjama-like uniforms, who
combed the ruins for the dead. It was so
customary that Müller didn't notice it
through the Gestapo HQ window any more.

*'Jawohl, Obergruppenführer!'* Heinz, a little
hunchback of a man who was his secretary,
answered in his hoarse deferential whisper.
He rubbed his bony hands – a gesture that
the head of the Gestapo detested – and
added, 'Naturally, he hasn't confessed to
being Jewish, Obergruppenführer.'

Gestapo Müller, as he was nicknamed
behind his back, grinned, showing the gold
teeth of which he was inordinately proud.
'Would you? In a place like this, Heinz?
Papers?'

Obediently, his secretary shuffled across

the regulation three paces distance which was stipulated in the rule book should separate a subordinate from a superior in the Secret State Police. He handed the documents over and Müller nodded as he noted the words stamped in red on them, *Secret State Matter: By Officer Only*. Obviously the captive Ami Yid was important. He'd have to keep his kid gloves on for this one. *At first, Heinrich, anyway*, a cynical little voice at the back of his brain hissed.

'They say, Heinz, that even Reichsführer SS Himmler went to visit him at first. A *Yid*!' He allowed himself a mild smirk, for he hated Himmler, his supreme boss, like he did most of those old Nazis, many of whom he had put behind bars in the old days in Munich before the Party had taken over. 'Even shook his hand, they tell me. A *Yid* at that!' Again he emphasised the cruel term.

Heinz looked to left and right as if he might be observed even in this place, and, lowering his voice, excused the Reichsführer SS with, 'In the line of duty, Obergruppenführer ... in the line of duty.'

Müller looked at the little worm. 'My dear Heinz,' he said in a patronising manner, 'don't you believe one shitting word of it. They're all making plans for the future. Even the Reichsführer.' His smirk broadened. 'Who knows when they might even need the Yid ... after all, he *is* disguised as an

Ami general.' He waved a big paw in Heinz's direction. 'All right, hop it! Tell them I'll be down in ten minutes ... in the cellars.'

Heinz gave an involuntary shudder at the mention of the cellars, and then, still wringing his bony hands, he disappeared as silently as he had come.

Müller switched on the red light outside his office door, which meant he didn't want to be disturbed under any circumstances, and then, opening the bundle of papers which had accompanied the prisoner from the Special Block of Sachsenhausen Concentration Camp, stared at the Jew's face. The photograph had been taken just after he had been captured in September on the German frontier, and he was still wearing Ami uniform with the one star of a brigadier general on his shoulders.

Müller sniffed. The man certainly didn't look like a general, even an Ami one. But he thought there was no mistaking the fact that the prisoner was a Jew. Not that he had anything against the Jews personally. In fact, he imagined his controller in Moscow was a Jew. It was just that as an old-time cop he was suspicious of everyone, and it wouldn't do for the Head of the Gestapo, as he was, to be seen as playing footsie with Jews.

Swiftly, he ran his thick sausage-like fingers through the papers, assimilating the basic facts about the unfortunate man

163

waiting for him below in the torture cellars of Number Ten. As always, he prided himself on his memory and the fact that he could assimilate and retain information so quickly. 'So,' he whispered, in the fashion of lonely men or those who have something to hide, 'born Kornfeld, Johann, in Cologne. Emigrated to States in '36.' He nodded as if in approval. 'Smart Jew. Seems to have joined the US Army early ... in '41. A patriot, eh?' Müller said aloud. 'Or a German-hater. Badges on uniform indicate the prisoner is ... *was* ... in US Intelligence. Attached to Eisenhower's staff...' Müller paused and gazed again out of the window at a bombed Berlin.

Two elderly men in the uniform of the great Berlin Zoo were carrying a stretcher solemnly. On it lay a great monkey of some sort. On its head there was a blood-stained bandage. But whoever had attempted to tend to the creature had been too late; the monkey was already dead. Müller grinned. The strange little scene seemed to him to sum up the whole stupid business of the dying Reich.

There was something going on between the Amis and some as yet unknown Germans, probably those *Monokelfritzen* of the General Staff again, who had failed to kill the Führer in July. Now the upper-class bastards wanted to save their own skins by doing a deal with the Amis. They'd do anything now to keep the war going in Russia, if the Western Allies would let them. Naturally, the fanatics around Hitler, Skorzeny and the like, would torpedo any deal of this kind. So it was up to him, the hated and despised Gestapo Müller, to scotch the deal if he could. Naturally, his bosses in Moscow were equally keen to do the same. They didn't want the Anglo-Americans to pull out of the war while the Red Army bore the brunt of the fighting.

Müller dismissed the strange little cortège below. He leaned back in his chair, sausage-like fingers pressed together in front of his cruel little mouth thoughtfully. It was funny, he told himself. Here he was, a humble little cop from Munich who had not risen above the rank of sergeant in his first fifteen years in the Bavarian police. Now, indirectly, he was influencing great political and strategic events, ones which might well change the fate of Europe for years to come.

The problem was to connect the Jew Kornfeld with these traitors of the so-called resistance. He smiled yet again. Another irony. A German Jew who had been forced to flee the country of his birth helping the same people who had been behind that personal tragedy and might even have been involved in the mass extermination of his co-religionists. In the name of the Third

Reich and its beloved Führer, he, Müller would ensure that the plot fell apart. Thereupon he would receive a fat salary, a secure position and a general's rank in the Moscow NKVD. A triple betrayal one might say.

The thought pleased him. He rose. Slowly he took up his cap and riding whip; that always helped to do the trick with the unfortunates down below in the cellars. 'A triple betrayal,' he whispered aloud to himself. 'Yes, I like that ... a triple betrayal.' He turned off the red light and went out, swinging his switch, as if he were setting off for a pleasant ride in a peace-time Tiergarten.

Kornfeld was not a brave man, but he was a determined and defiant one. He knew he had only to last till they took him back to the new cell they had given him here in Berlin. Once in there, he'd put an end to it all. He shrugged and wished next moment he hadn't. The initial roughing-up by the Gestapo thugs – part of the usual routine when changing prisons – made his skinny body hurt like hell.

He guessed that by now they had discovered the most important things about him: his name and the fact he was a Jew. They would have determined that as soon as they had stripped him immediately after his kidnapping. The Gestapo thugs thought that anyone who was circumcised was a Jew. In vain he had protested that many male

Americans were circumcised for hygienic reasons. But that didn't matter now; it was history.

What did matter, as far as the Gestapo thugs were concerned, was his role on Eisenhower's staff: a German Jew in American uniform, posed as a US general so close to the front. He knew they were suspicious and probably close to the mark. Now they were going to see if they could break him and find out the truth.

Kornfeld licked his cracked, bloody lips thoughtfully. That meant he had lost the protection of Himmler, the head of the SS, who had played patsy with him for a while, trying to sound him out on a separate peace with the West, in which he, Himmler, could play some role in a post-war German government.

Why, he didn't know, nor care at this juncture. His job was to protect the genuine Germans as long as he could. For he was under no illusions as he stared around at the bare walls of his tiny holding cell, its only furniture a concrete bed and the hole in the floor which served as a lavatory and which was totally useless for his purposes. The Gestapo torturers would make him talk in the end. No one could stand up to their brutal, sadistic methods for ever. What was it they usually boasted to their prisoners before they started working on them? *This is*

*X or Y* ... or whatever the thug's damned name was ... *They say he can get even an Egyptian mummy to talk.* And then probably they would laugh their damned heads off. Kornfeld shivered in spite of himself. For down the long corridor he could hear the stamp of heavy boots and the rattle of the turnkey's key. That was a warning for any prisoner and guard along that corridor to turn and face the wall in case they encountered another unfortunate. In the cellars of Number Ten Prinz Albrechtstrasse you entered and were never seen again, even by those like yourself who were already condemned to death.

The door was opened with harsh ceremony. First the turnkey, withdrawing each bolt with a hollow clang and turning the final key with a squeak. Then the harsh bellow, *'Tür offen, Obergruppenführer!'*

Kornfeld started at the rank. He was going to be examined by the top swine, and in the Gestapo such folk didn't like waiting for answers; they could turn even nastier than usual if they were kept waiting.

A couple of huge thugs entered and peered around the bare cell as if they half expected he had a machine gun waiting for them. Satisfied, they positioned themselves against the dripping concrete wall with their arms folded across their brawny, black-uniformed breasts, jackbooted feet spread.

168

Kornfeld ordered himself not to be impressed. He knew it was all part of the process of intimidation:

They were followed by a small group of middle-aged, fat men dressed in the uniforms of majors and colonels in the SS. They scowled and looked threatening. But their eyes gave them away. It was all a front. They were bored by the whole business. They had simply done it far too often before, and Kornfeld recognised them for what they were: experienced, old-time cops who would never have risen beyond the rank of sergeant if it hadn't been for the Nazis. Now they were officers in the feared SS. In reality, they were simply small-time bureaucrats serving their time until they qualified for a nice cushy retirement. He waited for the big shot.

Gestapo Müller didn't look much different from the rest. He was small, middle-aged and fat around the middle, with one of those shaven-headed Bavarian haircuts that left a tuft of dyed black hair at the front of his huge head. But his eyes were different from the rest. They were hooded, yet intelligent, and he had a strange trick, perhaps learned in order to intimidate his prisoners, of moving them rapidly from one side to another. Kornfeld felt an icy finger of fear trace its way slowly down the small of his spine. Gestapo Müller had to be watched.

But when Gestapo Müller opened the interrogation in his Munich accent his statement was banal, and as conventional as Kornfeld would have expected from the others. 'Jew Kornfeld, you'd better tell us the truth at once.' The eyes flashed from side to side, obviously to impress and frighten the prisoner. 'We have people here who could make an Egyptian mummy talk, like a yellow canary.' He gave a dry laugh and the others laughed dutifully, as if it were the greatest joke that they had heard in a long time. Müller thrust his big face close to Kornfeld's, so that the latter could smell his mixture of beery breath and expensive French eau-de-Cologne. 'You understand, Jew Kornfeld.'

'Yes, I understand, Obergruppenführer,' he replied, forcing himself not to move back and trying to keep his voice as steady as he could.

'*Gut. Dann verstehen wir uns.*'

Müller nodded to one of the ex-cops, now masquerading as a colonel in the SS, 'Walther.'

'*Jawohl, Obergruppenführer!*' the colonel barked and snapped to attention, as if he were a recruit on the parade ground. It was too regimented, too formal. Kornfeld would have laughed if he had been capable of doing so. But he wasn't, he was afraid. He admitted that to himself. This fat little man might be playing games at the moment, but they were games that might well have a deadly outcome for him. He waited tensely.

Walther slapped him across the face. His head snapped back. He had been caught by surprise. Walther's face had shown no sign that he was going to start like this. 'All right, Jew Kornfeld,' he said stridently, 'we know all about you. So, there is no point in lying. Tell us what we want to know and it'll be the better for you.' Again he slapped Kornfeld on the other side of his face and again he was caught by surprise.

Müller nodded his approval and, clearing his throat, asked in what the Germans called a *dezent* fashion, 'You had contacts here. Who are they, please?'

Kornfeld hesitated. He knew what would come when he did speak. But he had to face it, there was no other way. As if he knew he was already signing his own death warrant, he answered in a voice that he didn't quite recognise as his own, 'I demand to be treated as a prisoner-of-war. I know nothing of what you ask, Obergruppenführer.' He added his rank just in case it might help him.

It didn't. Walther lashed out with surprising speed for such a chubby, middle-aged man. His steel-shod boot caught Kornfeld on the left shin. He howled with pain. Instinctively, he doubled up. Before he could complete the movement one of the others hit him on the point of the chin, followed by another blow on his nose. The bone broke. Gobs of dark red blood splattered everywhere, including on Gestapo Müller's boots. Then they were all on him, as he collapsed against the wall, smashing their fists and boots into his defenceless body. The treatment had commenced.

# Two

'Skorzeny?' Müller asked over the phone. He made his voice non-committal, though he didn't like Hitler's blue-eyed boy, who had shot to fame after he had supposedly rescued Mussolini the year before. Skorzeny was one of those damned Austrians on the make, and all good Bavarians hated Austrians.

'Obergruppenführer,' Skorzeny said eagerly. 'Did you find out anything from that supposedly Ami general?'

Müller was too old a hand to give anything away for free. Casually, he remarked, 'This and that. You know he's a Jew ... a German Jew?'

'Yes, yes,' Skorzeny fell into the trap like the great big streak of Viennese piss that he was. 'I have received a report on that.'

Müller smirked. Naturally, Skorzeny also had his sources at Sachsenhausen Camp. 'You know his contacts in the Reich as well, I suppose,' Müller ventured carefully. 'Military, of course,' he took a chance.

'Yes.' Skorzeny was a little careful now, as Müller surmised that the big commando leader didn't know too much after all. 'I have some indications of who he wanted to speak to, and naturally you're right, they are military, of course.'

'Of course,' Müller echoed encouragingly.

'From our own sources, General Schellenberg' – Skorzeny meant the clever young head of the SS's own Secret Service, again a man whom Müller detested – 'and I have learned that perhaps General von Christiansen is the man behind all this treacherous business.'

Müller could have laughed out loud there and then. Christiansen was a senile, old, fat bastard, whose main interest in life, as far as he knew, was chubby-kneed, plump-behinded Hitler Youths. He would not know anything about political intrigue if it came up and hit him on his bald head with a club. But he didn't tell Skorzeny. Making his voice seem to display great interest, the Gestapo chief said, 'Now that *is* interesting. We here in Berlin have had some suspicions along those lines for some time now. Nice to see that you can confirm them.'

Skorzeny swallowed the ploy hook, line and sinker. 'We might be hairy-assed, old stubble-hoppers, Obergruppenführer,' he proclaimed, 'but we do keep our ears to the ground, you know!'

'We are honoured to have your assistance, Skorzeny,' Müller replied, tongue-in-cheek, wondering what the big Viennese cretin was talking about. Why couldn't he speak good, straightforward, simple German?

'Should I send a squad to have him arrested forthwith?' Skorzeny said enthusiastically. 'He's out on his estate in the country, weaving his treacherous spider's web. It would be no trouble.'

'No,' Müller said hurriedly, 'if you'll forgive me, Skorzeny, that's not the way to do these things. We need to allow the damned traitor to implicate himself more deeply in his devilish machinations.' He liked his own choice of words; they'd appeal, he was sure, to Skorzeny's simple mind.

'I follow you, Obergruppenführer.'

'Excellent, Skorzeny. For, you see, when we strike this time, we want to destroy the whole evil conspiracy once and for all. After this there will be no one throughout the Reich who will dare to make an approach to those Jewish gangsters, the Americans. Both sides, the Germans who wish to betray their country and the American seducers with their Jewish gold, must learn that this is an end to it. Germany will never surrender. Come what may, we will fight to the end.' He paused for breath and felt a fool at his choice of words.

Skorzeny, however, lapped them up. 'I

understand fully,' he snorted enthusiastically. 'Root them out for good!'

'Exactly, Jagdkommando. Now you must excuse me ... I must get back to the interrogation of the Jew Kornfeld ... And, by the way, brief me immediately on the Wotan plan as soon as the Obersturmbannführer returns from Aachen.'

'I will, sir ... I will,' Skorzeny said, and then Müller heard a small sharp noise, as if the giant Viennese fool was clicking his heels together as he stood to attention with the phone in his big paw. Next moment it came, almost deafeningly, *'Heil Hitler!'*

'Yes,' Müller was tempted to say, and add the old contemptuous greeting, 'Hail Hitler when you see him.' But, being the ultra-cautious man that he was, he snapped back, *'Heil Hitler!'* and put the phone down on its cradle with a resounding crash, as a good National Socialist bureaucrat should.

For a moment he sat there thinking. His thoughts weren't pleasant; they never were. But they pleased Heinrich Müller. For they fitted nicely into the cunning mosaic he was creating in his own mind. As he saw it, it didn't matter one damned iota who the traitors were within the Reich. As far as he was concerned, it could be that senile pervert von Christiansen. He was a general, an aristocrat, and he hated the Nazis. That was sufficient.

What did matter, however, Müller mused as he ran the matter through his devious mind, was that the Amis would never again attempt to approach would-be German plotters. They had to be shown that Germany would fight to the end. That would keep the Amis fighting, too, and help the Red Army in its take-over of a beaten Reich. After all, a victory for the Red Army would mean a general's job in Moscow and a nice fat pension afterwards to be spent somewhere on the Black Sea. He knew the Reds of old. They'd provide him with everything he needed as long as he remained discreet, even women; and he was getting decidedly sick of his wife and her damned daily masses in Munich, and of his secretary-mistress here in Berlin. A nice nubile Russian, who couldn't speak German but knew how to open her legs when called upon to do so, would suit him down to the ground.

Müller smiled at the thought. He could take to that kind of life without the slightest difficulty, living – as the German phrase had it – 'like the king in France', though in this case it would be in Russia.

He dismissed the future and concentrated once more on the present. It was clear that the Amis had to be taught a lesson, one which would teach them to avoid any further contact with this supposed German opposition, especially the high-level kind which Kornfeld had been trying to arrange. With whom, it no longer mattered. For the problem was no longer the German opposition, but the American would-be contacts.

He leaned back in the chair for a moment, fingers held in front of his thin slit of a mouth in that characteristic pose of his when he was thinking. Down below, the grave robbers were apparently too slow for their military overseer, or perhaps he was trying to impress any observer from the Gestapo HQ; for he had one of the convicts on the floor and was kicking him hard in the guts, regardless of the thick stream of deep-red, rich blood spurting from the wretch's gaping mouth. Müller hardly took in the scene of man's merciless cruelty to man. He had seen so much of it in the last few years that it barely registered.

By now Müller knew the location of the Amis' attempts at contact with the German opposition. It was Luxembourg, centered upon their great headquarters in the principality's capital city. He assumed that was why the SS raiding party had taken Kornfeld in that very area. He had been checking out the terrain. Then, the front had been very porous; now it was better manned on both sides, he had to admit. All the same, the area was so rugged and wooded that it wouldn't be too difficult for a German who knew that Eifel-Ardennes border region to get through it without being detected. And most German soldiers had been stationed there at one time or another.

So, the Amis assumed that any potential German traitor would make contact with them via that particular route. He sniffed. The man in the striped pyjamas in the gutter was moaning pitifully now, hardly attempting to ward off the cruel blows the overseer levelled at him. Casually, Müller registered that the convict would be dead soon if the guard didn't desist.

Slowly, a plan began to unfurl in his big head like a poisonous snake unwinding, ready to strike home with fangs filled with some deadly venom. What if they used Kornfeld as a decoy? And what if he succeeded in locating some Ami of importance on that remote frontier? And what if that important Ami suffered a sudden demise? And what if ... Müller's face broke slowly into a smile as the plan began to unfold itself, as if it had been ready-made in his brain all the time and had just needed to be recalled for it to be realised in its full beauty.

The only problem, as he saw it, was to find some indirect means to lure the prominent Ami negotiator into the trap. It couldn't come from the Germans involved, for at present they still wouldn't know who they were until Kornfeld spilled the beans. And the Jew was turning out to be tougher than they had anticipated. In the end they had beaten him into unconsciousness and they would have to wait some time before he recovered and was subjected to the next beating. He would undertake that himself, and this time Kornfeld would really spill his guts, or else!

But even if Kornfeld confessed, and even if he was prepared to play ball with them, he didn't trust him or his information. Like all Jews, Müller knew, Kornfeld would be cunning and unreliable. No, there had to be some other way of luring the Amis into the trap he wanted to set for them. *But what?* He hammered his big fist on the desk in sudden fury and frustration.

The knock on the door made him start. His problem was forgotten for a moment. He was angry. Didn't the fool know that he should never be disturbed under any circumstances when the red light glowed above the outside door. Was the fool blind?

'*Herein!*' he commanded angrily.

It was Heinz. His face was flushed as if he were in an advanced stage of galloping tuberculosis, and he was wringing his hands furiously as if he would never get them dry again.

'Heaven, arse, and cloudburst, man!' Müller burst out furiously. 'Are you shitting blind, eh! Didn't you see the red light?' He stopped short. The whole front of his

180

secretary's highly polished soft shoes – *brothel creepers*, he always called them to himself contemptuously – were a deep, wet red, as if they had just been dipped in a can of red paint.

'Obergruppenführer,' Heinz gasped, skinny, bony chest heaving as if he had just run a great race.

'Yes, yes ... come on, spit it out, man ... *Wo brennts?*'

Heinz swallowed and caught his breath. 'It's the Jew ... Obergruppenführer ... the Jew Kornfeld...'

'What about him, Heinz?' Müller rapped impatiently.

'He's just committed suicide, sir ... slit his wrists with a sliver of enamel from the cell piss-bucket. There's blood everywhere!' Heinz swallowed again hard at the memory and looked as if he might be sick at any moment.

Now it was Müller's turn to swallow hard. Now he knew what that red liquid on Heinz's shoes was. It was Kornfeld's blood.

# Three

Now things moved fast at the Gestapo HQ.

Müller went down to see the body before they stripped the corpse. Kornfeld must have suffered incredible pain as he had worked to kill himself with an SS guard only metres away from his cell door. One cry and naturally the guard would have stopped his primitive means of suicide. He had clawed a sliver of sharp enamel from the inside of his piss-bucket. A silent and somewhat impressed Müller, that is as far as the head of the Gestapo could ever be impressed by anything, could see how the ends of his fingers were cut and bloody, with the nails broken here and there as he had clawed the razor-edged piece of enamel free.

Then, stuffing his mouth with one of his socks so that if he were forced to scream with pain the noise would be stifled, he had systematically slit his wrists. Now there was blood everywhere – no wonder Heinz's shoes had been so red – growing thick and gelatinous in the freezing cold of the underground cell.

'For a Yid, pretty brave,' one of the old Gestapo hands commented. *'Sakrament!'* he cursed, half in admiration, half in wonder, 'the Yid even bit through his sock in his agony. Look, his lips are all bloody where he chewed them!'

'Perhaps he thought he'd have a last bite before he snuffed it,' another said heartlessly. *'Gefillte Fisch.'*

'Hold your trap!' Müller broke in. 'You're like a bunch of shitting old women.'

Automatically, the two old cops, both Bavarians like himself, clicked to attention. They were the usual timeservers and turncoats, who were sitting it out till their pensions came and they could put on their slippers permanently.

'Strip him. Check if he's got a *Kassiber* up his arse!' Müller rapped out his orders, not taking his eyes off the dead man curled in the foetal position around the piss-bucket, which was full of blood too. As he did so, he wondered at humanity yet again. They fought – and died – for things which at the time seemed of world-shaking importance, but which in a matter of days would be relegated to the forgotten moments of history. *Carrot and stick*, he told himself, *carrot and stick*: that was all life was about really.

He dismissed the thought, and as his underlings went to work he snapped at

Heinz, 'Come on, man, don't stand there like a fart in a trance, there's work to be done.'

There was.

Now Müller started to put his makeshift plan into operation. He felt a sense of urgency, for he had already realised that when Himmler and the plotter – whoever they were – realised that Kornfeld had been arrested, they would attempt to sabotage or delay whatever plan he, Müller, proposed. He didn't want that. He wanted the *action*, as Müller called it to himself, to be carried out swiftly and ruthlessly. It had to be an effective lesson so that the Amis would not dare to make any further attempts to contact the so-called German Resistance.

Naturally, Skorzeny would want to get into the business. He always poked his big Austrian nose into every thing that might be of some advantage to himself and his inflated reputation. Behind his back they called the big scar-faced freebooter, *the Führer's blue-eyed boy*. No, Skorzeny would find out what had been done once it had already taken place.

Still, the Gestapo had no troops of its own. They couldn't use the Wehrmacht. That would be too dangerous. There were too many loose tongues in the General Staff. The resistance would soon find out what was afoot. So, if he couldn't use Skorzeny's commandos and the Wehrmacht's assault squads, it had to be Himmler's Armed SS.

While the sirens shrilled their urgent warning that afternoon, indicating that the American Air Gangsters, as the Führer called them, were on their way again, Müller pondered the problem of the SS. Outside in the cluttered offices, teleprinters clattered, telephones jingled, staff ran back and forth carrying out orders, collating information, passing on instructions pertaining to the new emergency operation on the Western Front. In the end he made his decision, one that surprised Heinz, his secretary, who had long become accustomed to showing no suprise at whatever his boss did. 'Heinz,' he ordered, shortly before the US pathfinders arrived to start dropping their guide flares this grey November afternoon, 'we're off.'

'Off where, sir?'

'To the Eifel.'

Heinz looked aghast. 'But that's the front, Obergruppenführer!' Heinz exclaimed.

Müller allowed himself a lazy grin momentarily. 'Yes, I believe it is. The place where people get killed *suddenly.*'

The rest of the colour drained from Heinz's already pale face, and he wrung his hands furiously, as if they had suddenly become very soiled.

Müller's smile vanished.

'It's no use trying to travel by air. We'll use

the car. Air's too dangerous. Get to it, Heinz...' the rest of his orders were drowned by the first thunder of Berlin's massed flak guns. To the west the Ami *Christmas Trees*, great bundles of multi-coloured flares, started to drift down menacingly. Behind them came the massed formations of the enemy Flying Fortresses. Müller was right about the Berlin courier plane to the front. It was time to go before the Ami bombs cut off the road network westwards yet again.

But even as the great grey Gestapo Horch roared through the gathering gloom – the aircraft spotter, in his leather mask against the biting wind, scanning the skies for enemy Mustangs, which often broke off from escorting the bombers to attack targets on the roads and railways below – Müller kept on working furiously. It wasn't that he feared enemy interference, but that of Skorzeny, Himmler and the like plus those of the supposed German Resistance who might use those thickheads to delay the action he had in mind.

In essence, he urgently needed this young SS hero, von Dodenburg, who had been picked apparently by Skorzeny for clandestine ops behind the Ami lines. From his own records – Müller had records on virtually everyone and had made it a priority to keep them over the years since 1933 – and those kept by Heinz, he knew that this young SS daredevil had won every piece of tin that the Third Reich had to offer. His SS Assault Regiment Wotan was apparently known as the Führer's Fire Brigade, being rushed from one end of the front to the other to put out the blaze wherever the Führer decreed. That was why, apparently, the elite regiment, or what was left of it, had been shipped to a surrounded Aachen. Now the problem was where to find von Dodenburg and Wotan. As he had been ordered to do, von Dodenburg had pulled out his Wotan from the Aachen front without informing the Aachen Battle Commandant, Oberst Wilck. Thereafter, he had disappeared.

Half an hour after they had left a blazing Berlin, with Flying Fortresses falling out of the flak-pocked sky like great silver birds shot on the wing, he had radio-phoned an old acquaince, Sepp Dietrich, now commander of the 6th SS Panzer Army, to which Wotan belonged.

Müller got straight down to it, speaking in clear, though he knew just how dangerous that was. But time was running out and he was prepared to take that risk, 'Sepp, where's von Dodenburg's outfit?'

At the other end, Dietrich, a Municher like himself, gave his customary chuckle, seasoned by years of cheap cigars and even cheaper booze. 'You asking me, Heini?' he countered, using Müller's old nickname.

'You don't know him except for the news-papers. But that arrogant aristocrat bastard is a law unto himself. Even his army com-mander doesn't know half the things *he* does!'

'But he's supposed to be breaking out to our own lines in you-know-where,' Müller objected.

'He's supposed to do a lot of things,' Die-trich said, as if the phrase explained every-thing. He sighed like a man sorely tried. 'But if you knew him like I know him ... All right, I'll chase him up as soon as he deigns to make contact with his army commander ... *me*!'

'Fine,' Müller snapped, wondering yet again at the power of the Gestapo. Even army commanders such as Dietrich, old Party bully-boy that he was since the Munich days, were afraid of the Secret State Police. 'Keep in touch. I'm coming your way. Over and out.'

Again the big car plunged through the night, stopping at regular intervals while sentries on the roadblocks that were every-where – indicating an offensive soon to come – attempted to check their passes, until Müller flashed that fancy document, signed by the Führer himself, which had them jumping to one side and waving the Horch on as if they couldn't get rid of the Gestapo officials soon enough. The sight gave Müller a certain amount of satisfaction. It wasn't that it flattered his ego. It was more that it gave him a feeling of almost total security. It told him that even if anyone ever suspected him, there would be no one powerful enough, save the Führer himself, to do anything about it.

He leaned back in the comfort of the back seat and lit a small workman's cigar to soothe his nerves, which were jangling electrically with excitement at the plan he was working out to keep Germany in the war, secure in the knowledge that no one could stop him now. A few months more and this episode would be part of the secret history of World War Two, and he would be far away from a defeated, ruined Germany playing a new role as a Russian NKVD general. He smiled happily and closed his eyes.

He was awakened perhaps half an hour later by a harsh light being flashed into his eyes and Heinz saying urgently, 'Obergruppenführer ... Obergruppenführer ... wake up, please ... It's urgent.'

Müller was awake instantly. He blinked and shouted, 'Get that shitty light out of my eyes. Do you want to blind me?' He blinked again and things came into shadowy focus.

They had been stopped at another roadblock. This time it was a large one at the end of a bridge, with what looked like a platoon of helmeted Volkssturm – the German

Home Guard – picketing it, and from below Müller could hear the faint murmur of slow-running water.

'Alarm Company Trier!' An officer marched to the centre of the harsh white light and saluted. 'Roman Bridge Detachment.'

Müller grunted something and realised where he was. He was just about to cross the River Moselle at the ancient Roman-founded city of Trier. Up in the stark heights beyond was Luxembourg and enemy country. He was almost there. 'What is it?' He addressed Heinz. Police sergeant that he had been for so long, he had now learned that high-ranking persons never addressed subordinates like the Home Guard officer directly, but always through a second party. 'What's he want, Heinz?'

His secretary lowered his voice and started to rub his skinny hands, always a sign of nervousness in Heinz. 'Priority cable-signal, sir. From Prinz Albrechtstrasse.'

Now Müller was wide awake. This had to be important. To send a signal like that while the Horch was on the road must have occupied the attentions of a good couple of dozen officers. 'All right!' he snapped. 'Piss or get off the pot. Don't keep me in suspense.'

Heinz was a sensitive little man, but he knew he had to tolerate Müller's Bavarian crudity. He knew too much to ask for a transfer. Any show of disobedience and he'd end up behind *Swedish curtains*, as his boss liked to call prison bars, in the police fashion. He leaned forward, his mouth almost touching Müller's hairy ear – a closeness that was extremely distasteful to him – and whispered, so that the Home Guard officer couldn't hear, 'I've read it, sir. It's in clear...'

'Oh, for God's sake,' Müller interrupted impatiently. 'Get on with it, will you, Heinz?'

'Sir! Well, it's simple, Obergruppenführer. But it's what you ... *we* ... want,' he corrected himself hastily. 'The bait has arrived in Paris from London. One of our people spotted him at Orly last night at eighteen hundred hours and...'

'This nigger jazz music player?' Müller interrupted him harshly. 'The one who broadcasts to our soldiers in German?'

'Yes, that one, sir.'

'Anything else?'

'No, sir. Save that our source reports that he has gone to the American HQ at Fontainebleau.'

Müller gave his secretary a fleeting smile while the officer stared at the two Gestapo officers, wondering what kind of devilment they were planning.

Further off, one of the ancient Home Guardsmen – a dewdrop balanced at the end of his pinched, red nose – was saying,

'All right for them in their fancy car, Karl. But what about yer common-or-garden Folk Comrade. He ain't even had his shitty lung-torpedo ration fer this month.'

If Müller heard that cry from the heart of the common man, his *Folk Comrade*, he gave no indication. His broad, peasant face lit up. 'Heinz,' he said happily. 'The Amis have taken the bait. We've got 'em!'

Dutifully, Heinz echoed his boss's cry of triumph. 'Yessir, *got 'em* ... that we have, Obergruppenführer!'

It was only later – when the big, camouflaged Horch began to move slowly over the bridge which the Romans had built to defend this same frontier nearly two thousand years before – that Heinz remembered something that was missing from the equation: *Obersturmbannführer von Dodenburg and his reluctant heroes of SS Assault Regiment Wotan!*

# Paris
# December 1944

# One

Major Glenn Miller didn't know whether to be awed or repulsed. Paris – even a strained, wartime Paris – seemed another world, totally different from any other city he had ever known. It was certainly far removed from London, although that too was a European city caught up in the grip of total war.

There were troops everywhere, just as there were in London. But these men – mostly on leave, he guessed, from the AWOL bags they all seemed to carry with them, and which he suspected were filled with black-market goodies to sell to the civilians who hovered around them – were different. They looked wilder and many of them carried side arms, and virtually everyone appeared drunk. There were even those who staggered down the streets, arm-in-arm with whores or wolf-whistling the regular girls, who were carrying bottles of hooch. And the white-helmeted MPs, billy sticks already in their big hands, looked the other way. Paris looked, it seemed to Miller, a lot wilder than London, where drunks were hustled off to the stockade so as not to offend the Limeys with their antics. He guessed the reason was that most of these guys were straight from the front and were intent on having a good time in *Gay Paree* before they were sent back to the killing machine of the line.

'The boys look as if they're going to whoop it up tonight, Glenn,' Lt Haynes, who ran the band for Miller, commented happily.

Miller took his eyes off a GI who had pressed one of the short-skirted whores against a doorway opposite, and who by his rapid body movements indicated that he wasn't waiting for nightfall to *whoop it up*, and said, 'Yes, I'm surprised they get away with it like that. But I guess the MPs turn a blind eye. After all, those guys over there stand a chance of not surviving to Christmas, don't they, eh?'

His subordinate was obviously not interested in the men's future, or even whether they might have one. His mind was clearly on other things. 'I'm glad you brought up Christmas, Glenn,' he remarked. 'You know the big concert we have on Christmas Eve from Paris here? We're having some problems with the hook-up. Apparently the shortwave radio guys...'

Glenn Miller held up his hand impatiently and stopped him. 'Look, I'm worried first about another job I've got to carry out for the Big Boss.' He frowned hard and looked at the familiar figure across on the other side of the broad *allée* who was signalling him to tell the driver to stop.

'You mean Ike himself?'

Miller decided to ignore the question. As confused as he was by all this cloak and dagger stuff – as he believed they called it – he felt it wouldn't be wise to give away too much to his manager. All the band guys were loose-mouthed, especially if they were on the booze, which most of them were. As Haynes looked at him, puzzled, and then at the little man in US uniform waving at them from across the street, he felt himself once again totally out of his depth; in fact, he felt totally out of his depth altogether in Europe. It was a foreign world, and although people must have thought that – as a big time bandleader who had starred in two Hollywood smash hit movies – he should have felt at home anywhere, Glenn Miller knew differently. He was just a hometown boy at heart.

Smith shook his hand formally, as a somewhat red-faced Miller tried to take his eyes off the thighs of the Parisian girls flying by on their old cycles. He could have sworn he caught a glimpse of pubic hair and, shocked, he told himself the frog dame couldn't have been wearing panties.

Smith didn't seem to notice. 'Glad I caught you, Glenn,' he said, taking the Major by the elbow with new-found familiarity, and steering him to the jeep he had chained to a lamp a hundred yards or so away. 'Lucky to have bumped into you ... just like that!'

Suddenly Miller was angry. What did the little agent think he was, some small town hick? *Lucky to have bumped into me ... my aching back!* he exclaimed hotly. 'You were waiting for me, buddy.'

Smith gave a mock sigh. He beat his breast – not with any great passion, it must be admitted – and said, *'Mea culpa*, old chap, *mea culpa* ... I confess, you're right. It was all laid on. It's the kind of game we play.'

Miller was not appeased, not even by the sight of a ravishing blonde leaning low over the handlebars of a man's racing bike, showing plenty of breast, skirts billowing up with speed to display the ample charms of knickerless loins. Hotly he said, 'You guys might play those games, but Mrs Miller's son don't. Holy cow, Smith, I was a bandleader before I got into the Army Air Corps and, despite the uniform and the major's rank, that's what I am now.' He paused for breath, chest heaving as if he had just played a very strenuous riff.

Smith was totally unperturbed by the outburst. He fumbled in his pocket to find the key to unlock the chain, at the same time checking to see if all the tyres were still there. 'Got to watch jeeps like a hawk in Paree,' he explained. 'They go like hot cakes on the black market.' He lifted the hood and began to put on the distributor head which he had taken with him as another safety measure. Paris was packed with French and American black-marketeers, and American deserters living off their wits, and French whores.

Satisfied, he indicated that Miller should get in. Miller hesitated and Smith said gently. 'You know, I taught Latin at Philips Academy before Pearl Harbour. A real Mr Chips: horn-rimmed glasses, tweed jacket with leather patches at the elbows and a copy of the Latin poets under my arm all the time ... the whole private school teaching bit. Caspar Milquetoast in person. Butter wouldn't melt in my mouth.' He smiled fondly at the memory.

Miller was puzzled, but he realised that Smith was telling him about his past at one of those East Coast schools where America's moneyed elite sent their youth to be finished.

Smith slipped behind the wheel of the Jeep and turned on the engine. He nodded with approval when it fired. 'Nothing stolen,' he said. 'Thank God! Yes, Glenn, we are all something else now. Look at me ... Caspar

Milquetoast four years on. Now I've strangled men to death with these delicate pinkies o' mine, and other things worse than that. Oh yes, the Old Bard said something about time making cowards of us all and that sort of stuff. I began to change ... time and circumstances can make killers of even the mildest of...'

'What has all this got to do with me?' Miller cut in, hardly understanding a word of what Smith had just said, and feeling a damned fool because he hadn't. Smith was talking down to him, making him feel more of a rube than he was. That increased his annoyance even further. 'And picking me up like this. Christ Almighty, Smith! You know very well that I'm supposed to see the Supreme Commander – why, I don't know – this day. I was on my way to Versailles just now.'

'*Doucement ... doucement*, my dear Glenn,' Smith said soothingly as he pulled out – quite illegally – into a convoy of Red Ball Express trucks bound for the front and all driven by blacks. One of them immediately behind the jeep honked his horn angrily. Smith smiled and waved his free hand in greeting as if he had just bumped into an old and dear friend. 'Salt of the earth, our coloured compatriots. Eleanor' – he meant the wife of President Roosevelt – 'dearly loves them.'

Miller snorted.

Smith continued. 'In this business, Glenn, we never do the expected. Ten minutes or so ago, you thought that big-mouth Haynes was taking you to Versailles to see Ike. That was as good a cover story as we could think up for you once we knew you were spending the night at the Orly Bachelor Officers' Quarters.'

Miller looked as if he might say something, then he closed his mouth, perhaps telling himself he ought to listen rather than protest. It might serve him better.

Next moment Miller felt he should have opened his mouth and said something, for the mysterious little man he called Smith announced calmly, 'No, we're not off to see Eisenhower at Versailles. We're going instead to the Sphinx to meet someone else.'

'The *Sphinx*?'

'Yes, a rather fancy cathouse. Thought you might have heard of it. All the best people go there.' And, with that, Smith concentrated on the traffic.

Naturally, in his time and due to his occupation, Glenn Miller had seen plenty of cathouses. He'd even played in a few in his youth. Swing music, black musicians, booze and cathouses went together. But that didn't mean he liked them. He felt they were really places meant for lowlife types. Besides, he knew you could easily catch certain *social diseases* in dives like that, even though the cheap pimps and crooks who ran them insisted that their dames were regularly inspected by medical doctors with letters after their monikers.

But the Sphinx *was* different. There was nothing gaudy about the place. Indeed, Miller wouldn't even have guessed the place's function if Smith hadn't told him that it was a whorehouse. Now they entered the salon, led by a negro dressed up in powdered white wig, silk knee stockings and a kind of eighteenth century coat with plenty of imitation gold buttons and lace ruffs. It was quite busy. There were Allied officers, mostly Americans of the rank of colonel, though Miller did spot a one-star brigadier general with a young WAC, which seemed strange. Why bring another dame to a place full of dames, women of all sizes, colours and nationalities. They all had one thing in common, though: they all had greedy eyes and an unwritten sign on their powdered foreheads. It read, *Money*.

Smith nodded to one or two, and for a man who maintained he'd been a school-teacher at one time or another, he seemed to be very familiar with the staff and at ease in the salon, which was decorated with portraits of naked women, some of them doing embarrassing things – at least, they were to Miller – to each other in graphic, loving detail.

'Crotch art at its finest,' Smith commented on one spectacular view of a well-endowed woman, nude save for a large hat, with her legs spread. 'Madame insists it was done by Dali in his masturbatory period.' He sniffed. 'I wonder?'

Miller said nothing. He couldn't. He was red with embarrassment

Smith took him by the arm. 'We shall go into a side-room. There's an exhibition going on, though I can't promise you the celebrated lady with the donkey.'

Miller looked aghast. He thought that kind of absolute decadence only took place in banana republics like Mexico. 'Christ on a crutch!' he cursed to himself. 'No wonder the wise guys cracked that the frogs could only make love with their lips. What a world!' Finally he managed to ask, 'But why here?'

Smith laughed cynically. 'My dear chap,' Smith declared – and now Miller thought the little Intelligence man sounded very British, and not at all the Yank he purported to be – 'when a fellow's got sex on his mind, he has no thought for the great affairs of mankind. What better place to talk about such secret matters than here?'

It was an explanation that Miller couldn't quite fault.

The room, although it was high-ceilinged

and there extractor fans, was blue with smoke, so that Glenn Miller started coughing immediately he entered. No one took a bit of notice. He could see why. On the raised stage, flanked by a small orchestra, there was a large drum. Over it squatted an enormously fat woman, nearly naked and greased with either sweat or oil. She had her fat thighs spread as far as they would go and, with beads of sweat dripping down her furrowed brow like opaque pearls, she was trying to suck up what looked like a large can while an absolutely intent and silent audience of middle-aged officers and the like watched in rapt awe.

'Holy cow!' Miller began, but didn't finish.

'Exactly,' Smith said quietly as he found a table in the corner, already occupied by a solitary figure muffled in a trenchcoat which looked vaguely military. 'It's taken from an English show – BBC – *Penny on the Drum*, I think they call it. Kinda request programme.'

'But the fat lady?' Miller stuttered, confused, as with a wet sucking motion the naked whore made what he now recognised as a two pound can of GI coffee disappear inside her. Suddenly he felt sick.

'Simple,' Smith answered. 'What she can take up, she keeps. That can of coffee is probably worth twenty dollars American on the black market.'

'Twenty-five outside Paris,' the shadowy figure in the battered trenchcoat interrupted.

Smith wasn't surprised in the least. He said, 'I stand corrected, old boy.'

On the stage, someone had tossed a collection of compo ration packets on the drum to the accompaniment of loud music by the little band. The whore pulled a face as if she just couldn't cope any more. Then she breathed out hard, her hanging breasts sliding down her fat greased body as she did so and started to squat once more.

'Jesus H Christ,' Miller breathed, and next to him the man in the trenchcoat whispered hoarsely, 'It's a pleasure to meet you, Major Miller. Shall we get down to business?'

# Two

'Well, I'll go and piss in the wind!' Schulze exclaimed angrily as he peered through the falling snow, down at the crossroads below. *'Amis!'*

Next to him, Matz – his ragged uniform soaked, his pinched, wizened face blue with cold – replied, 'Well, it ain't the frigging Salvation Army, Schulzi.'

His old running mate ignored the unnecessary comment. His mind was racing. Down at the base of the hill, dispersed among the snow-heavy firs, was what was left of SS Assault Regiment Wotan. Now they were in sight of the German lines and safety, just across the other side of the Luxembourg border, the river Sauer. But the Sauer could have been on the moon at this moment, for as soon as the Amis down there spotted the Wotan troopers, they'd make mincemeat of them plodding slowly down the hillside in the knee-deep new snow. 'Sauer by name and shitting sour by nature,' the big NCO hissed bitterly to no one in particular.

'Sweet Jesus!' Matz said, 'now yer frigging well talking to yersen, Schulzi. The men with the rubber hammers'll be coming along soon to take yer off to the funny-farm.'

'Shove it!'

'Can't, old house, got a double-decker bus up there already,' Matz said, being his usual comic self.

Schulze didn't respond. Instead he grunted, eyes narrowed against the cruel, beating snowflakes.

Matz saw the look. 'Perhaps they'll go home to shelter from the snow. You know the Amis. They stop the war when it rains and the like.'

'Not that little lot,' Schulze said. 'They've nested themsens in ... and the arseholes have got machine guns set up to left and right flank. See, at ten o'clock and over there at three o'clock.'

Now it was Matz's turn to be gloomy. 'Yes, you're not wrong there, old friend. It's a damned strong position. They'd need a bit o' winkling out. We'd take casualties trying.'

Schulze took out his binoculars and, shading the glass with one hand just in case some glint of bright light gave him away, he surveyed the American roadblock and the surrounding area leading down to the river and safety.

The Amis, he had to admit, had done a

good job. They had cleared the timber all around their position to a depth of a hundred metres, so that they had a completely free field of fire. All around them at the road, there stretched snow-covered fields. Any attacking infantry would be served up to them down there as if on a silver platter. The only alternative was to outflank them, and then – when it was safe to do so – make a quick dash for the river and hope for a swift crossing.

But there was a catch. In winter the Sauer was still shallow, but was quick-flowing, and Wotan was hampered by the wounded they had already incurred during their break-out from a dying Aachen.

Matz seemed to read his running mate's thoughts. For he broke the heavy, brooding silence with, 'Any other mob and they'd say a few kind words to the wounded, leaving 'em a couple of fags to smoke, and do a bunk. Not von Dodenburg's Wotan. The CO wouldn't allow it.'

'Yes,' Schulze agreed, 'the Old Man would never abandon the wounded, even to the Amis.'

He spat almost angrily into the snow and lowered his glasses. 'Fuck this for a game o' soldiers. There's got be another way...'

Fifty metres or so below, von Dodenburg had already sensed that they had come to some sort of dead end which could only be dealt with if he abandoned the wounded. But after Aachen, he didn't even trust the Amis. Like the Ivans – he meant the Russians, who always shot SS prisoners – they might well do the same at this present moment of tension and stress. No, there had to be a way forward and across the Sauer, one that included the wounded. But what?

Even as he slumped there in the snow, wet, hungry, worn-out and not a little miserable, the radio set buzzed faintly into life once more. The radio operator put on his earphones as von Dodenburg leaned over wearily and took the other set. It was the same voice as before, faint but recognisable. The message was in clear, but camouflaged by obscure references. In essence, however, it read 'Report immediately ... Urgent, report immediately ... *Führerbefehl* ... Hitler's Orders.'

In sudden anger, von Dodenburg snapped, 'Turn the damned thing off, signaller! I can't stand another *Führerbefehl!*'

'Yessir,' the young, frozen-faced signaller said, and turned off the radio. It went dead immediately, leaving behind a sudden silence, broken only by the howl of the snow-laden wind and the faint moan of the kid who had been shot in the guts by an incendiary slug and was dying.

Von Dodenburg pulled up his collar and tried to control his trembling. Obviously, he and what was left of his shattered command were needed back at Dietrich's HQ urgently. He could understand that. Under present circumstances, with the Reich falling apart, the old Party bully-boy needed every body he could rouse. All the same, it was clear to the young commander once again that the *Prominenz* didn't give a damp fart about the men. They were expendable. They were needed to die for *the cause*, whatever that was this winter of 1944.

He looked around at his beardless heroes and the odd remaining old hare – who looked, with his heavy beard, like their father – and told himself that these boys were Germany's future. Once – indeed ever since they had been in the short pants of the Hitler Youth – they had been taught there was nothing more noble than to die for Germany. Now he would have to teach them that it would be much better for the new Germany that would follow the death of the Thousand Year Reich which the Führer had boasted about so often and so pompously, if they learned to *live* for their homeland. Von Dodenburg swore grimly to himself as the snowflakes buffeted his hard, lean face with renewed force.

'Sir?'

Von Dodenburg woke from his momentary reverie. 'Yes?'

'It's Sergeant Schulze and Corporal

Matz.' He looked at the young panzer grenadier acting as sentry and then flashed a look up the snowbound hill to his rear.

The two rogues were ploughing through the deep snow in a hurry, the wind whipping the snowflakes around their bodies so that at times they seemed to vanish in the virtual white-out. At another time, von Dodenburg told himself, the two in this setting would have made a beautiful Christmas card: one of those typical Bavarian ones with the peasants returning on the afternoon of Christmas Eve, bearing the traditional fir tree they had just cut in the forest for the children's *Bescherung*. But not now. The two of them were slithering and sliding down the snowbound slope in too much of a hurry. This was war and they obviously had an urgent message to pass on. Von Dodenburg nodded to the sentry, 'Pass the word, Rottenführer. Everyone stand to ... ready to move out at five minutes' notice.'

'Sir!' The sentry staggered away against the howling wind to carry out the orders.

Panting, the two NCOs slumped down without greeting next to the CO. Von Dodenburg could see they were about all-in. They had both been towers of strength during the break-out, cajoling, threatening, encouraging the young troopers, carrying two or three rifles on occasion, and sometimes their owners as well. Now they were

211

about done. Hastily, he whipped out his silver hip-flask, presented to him by no less a person than Reichsführer SS Himmler himself. 'Here,' he ordered, 'have a drink!'

Schulze, surprisingly for such a notorious sauce-hound, hesitated.

'Go on,' von Dodenburg encouraged him. 'You and Matz need it.'

Matz licked his chapped lips, 'Do my tonsils a world of good,' he ventured, and before Schulze could refuse again – though that was very unlikely – he seized the flask and took a tremendous slug, his faded eyes watering with the impact of the powerful alcohol. Then, wiping the neck with the edge of his ragged sleeve, he handed the flask to Schulze with unwonted decorum, stating in his best German, 'Pray take a sip, Sergeant Schulze ... Do, for my sake.'

'*A sip!*' von Dodenburg echoed, hardly believing his own ears.

A few minutes later, their cheeks glowing now from the strong, rough German *Kognak*, Schulze had drawn out his bayonet and marked a circle in the snow at their feet. He dissected it and explained, 'The Ami position and the crossroads. Good field of fire for them all around. Useless for us to try to cross it with the wounded.'

Von Dodenburg nodded, but said nothing. Most commanders of his rank and experience wouldn't have let themselves be briefed by a lowly NCO. But von Dodenburg knew Schulze. The big non-com knew more about battle and infantry tactics than the generals who wrote training manuals on such matters.

'So,' Schulze went on, 'we'll have to outflank 'em .... either on the left or right. There's some cover. But not too much. If we were quick, we'd manage it. But with the wounded...' he shrugged his big shoulders and left the rest unsaid.

Von Dodenburg considered for a moment. 'The only way?'

'The only way, sir,' Schulze echoed with a note of finality. Next to him Matz nodded his head with due solemnity.

'All right. What's your suggestion?'

'Blind 'em by bullshit, sir!'

'How?'

'A feint to one flank, a real push to the Sauer on the other.'

'But we'll split our force. We'll weaken the *Schwerpunkt*.' Von Dodenberg meant the key point of attack. 'Might fail on both flanks that way.'

Schulze looked at his nails with mock modesty. 'Under normal circumstances, sir, I'd agree.'

'But under other circs?'

'With me and Matz here – that Bavarian barnshitter – doing the feint, it'll succeed all right, *or else*.' He looked at his old comrade in a threatening manner.

Matz simpered in what he took to be a female voice, 'Oh, Sergeant Schulze, you are so masterful ... you'll have me wetting me knickers in half a mo!'

Von Dodenburg laughed. There was nothing else he could do. Yet again he thanked God for the two rogues and all the rest of Wotan's old hares.

'But, just the two of you?' he queried.

'Well, sir, we *are* Schulze and Matz.' He made the statement as if that was explanation enough. Then, before the CO could object, he added, 'We'll need the last mortar and a couple of smoke bombs if there are any left.'

'There are.' Von Dodenburg knew a good commander should always know the state of his outfit's ammunition. He knew his. 'Six, to be exact, in the usual carrier.'

Schulze nodded. 'Even this little apeshit can manage them.'

Matz nodded loyally, ignoring the insult.

'But what about the tripod and tube?' von Dodenburg objected. 'Usually need two men to carry those.'

'I know I'm a bit weak on the breast,' Schulze said with mock modesty, 'but I think I could manage them.' He hesitated. 'Perhaps I'd need another sip of strong waters, however. Just to keep up my strength, though.' He licked his parched lips

214

in anticipation.

'Holy cow!' von Dodenburg said, half in admiration, half in exasperation. 'Schulze, one of these days you'll be the shitting death of me!'

Schulze frowned abruptly. 'I wouldn't say that, sir, please. We don't want to paint the devil on the wall, do we?'

Von Dodenburg nodded and then he forgot the warning and concentrated on getting the little attack on the road. Up on the hill the snow continued to come down in solid white sheets, as if it would never end and would bury this miserable war-torn country under its heavy mantle for good.

# Three

'I hope you're not squeamish at the sight of death, Major Miller?' asked the man in the trenchcoat, who had still not introduced himself. They were trudging through the mud and the melting snow towards where the blacks were busy at their morbid task as yet more trucks came skidding and slithering across the wet fields, carrying their cargoes of death. 'Meat wagons, the GIs call them,' the man in the trenchcoat explained as the two-and-a-half-ton truck nearest them upended its cargo in a flurry of stiff arms and legs to where the Negroes were waiting. 'Not exactly the most delicate of phrases, but' – he shrugged a little carelessly – 'what can you expect of them? They live with death all around them, poor sons-of-bitches.'

'I say,' Smith said, his English accent getting stronger, 'you've just created a *bon mot*, old chap! *They live with death all around them.*'

The man in the trenchcoat didn't comment and Miller told himself he was dealing

216

with crazy men, all of them. The whole of frigging Europe was mad. How he longed to be back home worrying about the next session, the expensive house he was building, his golf handicap! Instead, he had suddenly transported from a brothel to a burial ground here in the wilds of Northern Belgium. Why, he didn't know. And all the other two would tell him was, it was *on the orders of the Supreme Commander ... very hush-hush, you know.*

Near him, the blacks were beginning to carry away the dead from the front. One of the poor bastards had lost his head and both his hands. Perhaps a mine or something had exploded underneath him. Miller didn't know and didn't care. He felt the hot, bitter bile rise in his throat. With difficulty he controlled it just before he started to vomit.

Smith noticed his sudden, green paleness and said unfeelingly, 'Imagine what the non-com who has to process him feels like, Miller.' There was an abrupt sharpness in the ex teacher's voice, as if he were enjoying Miller's discomfiture and the knowledge that this soft bandleader – the darling of Hollywood and the Big Brass, eager for personal publicity – was finally realising what the shooting war was really about death in its most violent and unpleasant form.

The man in the trenchcoat took up the

processing business. 'You see, the blacks sort out the stiffs. They dig the holes and bury 'em. Well, first, they break off one ID tag for records, and the other is put inside their mouth and the jaws clamped down, so that when they're exhumed for proper burial later, the Graves Registration guys will know the name of the stiff they have dug up.'

Miller managed to utter a weak 'I see'. He daren't open his mouth very wide in case he couldn't control his guts and vomited. These days he had to be careful about everything he said or did. The papers would get anything bad and publicise it. He had to think of his post-war career.

'The worst job is that of the white sergeants at the sorting tables over there.' He indicated a line of rough, wooden US Army trestle tables upon which rested bloody remains without human shape looking like bundles of abandoned rags. Miller shivered at the sight. 'They try to get some identification from those awful bits and pieces you can see. You know, a shell does some awful rotten things to the human body. If they're lucky, they've got a head to check with the stiff's dental records back home in Washington. If the stiff doesn't have a head – and a lot of them don't – it's the fingerprints. But how do you get a print from a waterlogged hand? So they pump the fingers full of a special liquid. This raises the ridges, and if they're darned lucky they'll get a print. But if the stiff doesn't have hands either, they have a problem ... *and then some*, Major.'

Gently, Smith interrupted the other Intelligence agent. 'Sir, I think Major Miller has had enough of the horrors for the time being, don't you? Besides, what he's going to see next, if he's unlucky, won't be particularly pleasant either.' He smiled carefully at the other man, while Miller wondered what worse horrors there could be.

'Yes, I guess you're right. Let's move on, then.'

Leaning against the sudden flurries of icy snowflakes, which seemed to be coming straight from Siberia and made the three of them walk with their heads bent to prevent them from being blinded, they fought their way to a collection of rough wood-and-brick structures at the end of the fields. They dodged another meat wagon filled high with dead, their limbs flopping up and down with the vehicle's jerky motion, as if the dead were waving to them. They stopped outside the first rough hut. It bore the red cross of the US Medical Corps and the stencilled warning in big, black letters: *Keep Out! No Entry Without Special Authority!*

The man in the trenchcoat knocked. Nothing happened. He knocked again.

Then, inside, a chair scraped audibly as if there had been someone just inside the door all the time. A bolt was pulled back and an MP stood there, carbine slung over his shoulder, .45 pistol dangling from his waist and tied around his thigh with a leather thong. He looked like a caricature of some western movie gunslinger.

Smith grinned. Miller looked discomfited. But the man in the trenchcoat pulled rank immediately in his no-nonsense manner. 'Open the damned door, man, and let us in. It's freezing out here. Move it!'

The MP – abruptly realising that, despite all the gear and the white-lacquered MP helmet, he was still outranked – *moved it*, mumbling, 'Yes, sir ... at once, sir!'

They strode in, scattering wet and snow everywhere, even on the chair on which the guard had been resting his feet over the glowing, pot-bellied coal stove which heated the place. 'Where's the pathologist?' the man in the trenchcoat demanded.

'Path...' the MP stuttered a little helplessly. 'You mean the doctor, sir?'

'Yessir. Where?'

Abruptly, the tough-looking, officious MP crumbled into a cringing wreck. He pointed a finger at the next door, also marked *Keep Out* and quavered, 'He's down in there, sir. He's cutting up them stiffs, sir.'

Smith grinned sympathetically and, urging

Miller forward behind the other agent – who was already opening the door so that a great whiff of ether and other chemicals assailed their nostrils – whispered, 'Prepare for the worst, Major. This is also going to be unpleasant ... *very*, I'm told.'

'Thanks,' Miller answered, feeling as shaky as the MP looked, though he didn't know why he should thank Smith. But then at that particular moment he didn't know very much at all, save that he wanted to get out and back to Paris – decadent as it was – as soon as possible.

A tall skinny man in a blood-stained rubber apron and rubber boots was standing next to a running tap. In the basin there was something pale pink and obscene. The doctor – which was obviously what he was from his gear – took the scalpel and whipped it very swiftly across the pink object. 'Good to see you,' he said cheerfully, 'Won't be a moment. I'm just examining the gullet and trachea for signs of vomit.' He bent over his work, adding, 'I'll just do the tongue to check for internal bruising, if you don't mind. Then I'll be right with you.'

Miller couldn't stand any more. He turned, trying to stifle the terrible, hot gagging. To no avail. Before he could react he had bent and was retching vomit on the concrete floor. 'No matter,' the doctor said, without looking up from his autopsy. 'Often happens

... One of the darkies can sweep it up later.'

A few minutes later he was finished. He rose with a slight groan, as if his back hurt, and declared, 'All normal.' He pulled a round object out of the sink, dripping red liquid, and deposited it with a squelching sound in the metal tray to his right.

It was a human head, with the throat cut out, the mess of congealed, pinkish dust indicating to Smith – who knew something of these things – that the pathologist had worked on the corpse's head with a bone saw.

The doctor pulled off his rubber gloves with a slapping sound and, rubbing the circulation back into his bony hands, explained, 'We're always on the lookout for gas, you know. The Top Brass are shit-scared the Krauts might use it at this stage of the war. Any stiff brought in here with anything that might indicate that he's suffered death by some sort of gas poisoning, I do the works on him...' He paused and thrust out his hand, still white with the French chalk he had used to ease on the surgical glove, 'Why, Mr Miller himself ... er, *Major* Miller. How swell of you to come. I've always been a fan of yours, ever since I was a freshman at Yale.'

Miller hesitated. Smith nudged him. He obliged. He took the hand in the same instant that he saw that the top of the dead man's head had been excised and lifted on a skin hinge like a Fabergé egg. He couldn't control himself. He went back into the corner in a crazy rush and vomited yet again, while the three men stared at him as if he were a very peculiar creature indeed. Finally, the pathologist said, 'Perhaps a shot of bourbon might do the trick, what, gentlemen?'

It certainly stopped the vomiting, but it didn't stop Miller's hands from shaking like a leaf as they sat in the doctor's office with the wind howling outside and hail now pattering the window like showers of pebbles. Still, Miller was grateful for the drink. At least, every time he felt the heaving begin, threatening the vomit soon to follow, a sip of the powerful spirit controlled the movement and he could relax again for while.

'Well,' Smith asked – taking his time with his drink, though the other man, who was obviously his superior, was in a hurry – 'what does he look like?'

'You mean our Mr X ... or should I say, *Herr X*?' the doctor answered with a slight smile. 'Good, on the whole. It would take a thorough pathological examination on their part to spot what had really happened. The basic problem was the mark on his neck, but they hadn't let him swing the requisite, or perhaps he had bent his legs and pushed against something to shorten the fall. So the burn mark wasn't so pronounced and I managed to get rid of most of it with a few chemical dodges...' He stopped abruptly when he saw the puzzled look on Miller's pale face. 'Sorry, Major. But that was typical pathologist chatter. You know, they sit on stools all day examining other people's stools, as the old medical student's adage has it.' He smiled winningly at the band-leader.

Once more Miller was totally out of his depth, and sick with it. Perhaps it was those two factors which made him snap with unaccustomed force and anger, 'I don't give a fuck for medical students' jokes, or anyone else's for that matter!' He threw a nasty glance at Smith, who he felt was always making fun of him behind his back, and sometimes to his face, too. 'I was asked to come over here to play for the boys, which I've done ... at some considerable financial loss. Then I was asked to broadcast my stuff to the Krauts, which I've done and am still doing. Now I'm in this God-awful place in the middle of nowhere, right up at the front.'

'Not exactly, Major,' the pathologist interrupted gently, 'or I wouldn't be here either.'

Miller, two twin spots of hectic red flushing his pale face now, ignored the interruption. 'Mixing with hundreds of stiffs, not knowing whether I'm on my ass or my head...' His voice rose even more. 'I demand to know what's going on. Or,' he stuttered, gasping for breath, chest heaving with the effort, 'you can count me goddam out!' He glared around at the other three as if he expected to see some momentous reaction on their faces. If he did, he was disappointed. For they stared back at him in wonder, as if they couldn't understand what all the fuss was about.

'Major Miller,' the man in the trenchcoat said very formally after a moment's silence, 'you are here because you are a soldier under orders, let's not forget that. You have been *told* to be here by your superior officers.'

Miller's mouth dropped open stupidly. He had been caught out completely by the other man's outburst. Besides, no one had spoken to him like that since he had been a kid in grade school. For a few moments he spluttered and stuttered like a stranded fish, 'But I ... I ... only ... want to ... duty ... to do my duty, sir.' To his surprise he found himself addressing the man in the trenchcoat as if he were his superior. Perhaps he was. Miller never lived to find out. 'That's all. But sir, you must understand, I'm bewildered ... I don't know about these things, sir,' he ended lamely.

Abruptly, the other three were all sweetness and light. 'Of course, Major,' Smith said, while the pathologist leaned over and, without being asked, poured Miller another drink, making soothing *tut-tut* noises as he did so, like a family doctor might with an upset child. For his part, the man in the trenchcoat said, less harshly now, 'You see, Major Miller, we're playing for big stakes in this matter ... perhaps for some of the biggest in the whole of the war in Europe. Naturally, we can't reveal our hand *fully*, even to you...' He hesitated momentarily. 'But you can take it from me and my colleague' – he indicated a now smiling Smith – 'that you are about to play a great role in – if we strike it lucky – in ending the war here.'

'So,' Smith took up the conversation, 'if we can't tell you everything we know, you must understand it's for a very good reason indeed.' He turned to the doctor once more and said, 'So, Herr X will do, doctor?'

'I should think so,' the pathologist replied. 'I don't see why the Krauts should suspect anything. Besides, as you see it, he won't remain in the hands of the...'

He broke off suddenly. From outside there came the abrupt shrilling of whistles, cries, shouts of alarm; muffled by the snowstorm, but definitely there. The man in the trenchcoat sat up. Next to him, Miller, jerked out of his puzzled, chastened mood, cried,

'What in Sam Hill is going on?'

In that instant the door was flung open. A military police sergeant, carrying a carbine and looking as if he were ready to use it at any moment, blundered in, scattering snow everywhere and shouting, 'Sorry to disturb you gents. But there's a red alert just come in.'

'Red alert?' the doctor echoed. 'Why, Logan?'

'Krauts ... Krauts been spotted behind our lines down by the Sauer. Listen!' He turned his helmeted head to one side, as if indicating they should do the same. They did. Now they could hear the faint boom of what might be artillery and the firework crackle of what had to be a small arms fight to the east. 'Holy Christ,' the MO snapped, 'You're right!'

'Yessir! Now, let's move it, sir. Higher HQ just signalled that I've got to get you, these gentlemen and ... er ... your gear out of here toot-sweet.'

'Toot-sweet it is,' the pathologist echoed almost cheerfully and sprang to his feet. 'Come on, Major Miller, we have to move it. We want you to go on playing that beautiful horn of yours for a long time to come, don't we?' He took Miller by the arm and steered him urgently to the door as if he really meant it. But Major Miller would never play that beautiful horn of his again...

# Four

'Great crap on the Christmas Tree!' von Dodenburg moaned as he stared at the legless trooper writhing and thrashing out his death throes in the circle of blackened, smoking ground. The minefield had caught him and the rest of Wotan by surprise as they tried to outflank the Amis. He, in particular, hadn't expected them to prepare their defences so thoroughly. Normally the Amis were very careless about such things, or lazy. Now he had been caught out, and already the Americans were beginning to react. It was their typical reaction, massive and wasteful bursts of machine-gun fire mixed with other arms. They blasted away without aiming, but then, von Dodenburg knew they had plenty of ammo, and even undirected fire was dangerous at close quarters.

'Spread out!' he called. 'For heaven's sake spread out!' He raised himself from the cover of a snow-heavy hedge and blasted away with his Schmeisser, while here and there old hares supported him by tossing stick grenades in the direction of the nearest American machine-gun post.

But even as he reacted, von Dodenburg knew it was imperative that they must not get bogged down in a fire-fight here on this virtually coverless hillside. Time and reserves were on the Amis' side. They had to keep moving towards the Sauer before the enemy whistled up more men.

'Keep moving, men,' he cried above the lethal noise of war. 'Come on, follow me, the captain's got a hole in his arse!' Whether they heard the old, familiar cry or not, von Dodenburg didn't know. But by now most of them were up on their feet again and moving, urged forward by the snarling old hares, who obviously frightened them more than the Amis. But still they were taking casualties and their eyes were full of fear as they looked for the tell-tale triple wires of anti-personnel mines poking through the snow carpet. Von Dodenburg said a fervent, silent prayer and, like a sheepdog urging on his frightened charges, kept them moving.

Some two hundred metres to the right on the other flank Matz and Schulze, bent low under the great weight of the mortar tube and tripod heard the snap-and-crackle of the small-arms fire, too. They didn't need a crystal ball to realise what had happened. The rest of Wotan had run into trouble. Old hares that they were, they wasted no words.

With Matz squeaking after him, the hinge to his wooden leg as rusty as ever, Schulze plunged forward through the knee-deep, virgin snow to find a suitable position to fire upon the Amis before it was too late. He found it. A hollow surrounded on three sides by fringes of the fir forest, with the one facing the enemy open. He slammed down the heavy mortar tripod. Effortlessly, as if it were a child's toy, he rammed the legs into the snow till they reached the solid, frozen earth below. He grasped and picked up the mortar. With trained fingers, frozen as they were, he attached the tube and wound home the screws as Matz came up gasping with a case of mortar bombs in each hand. 'Where was you?' Schulze snarled, not looking up from his task. 'Thought I'd have to send you a frigging written invite if you was much later.'

'Shit in the wind!' Matz panted and, dropping the cases, started prising the cover off the cardboard tubes which contained the mortar bombs.

'All right, arse with ears,' Schulze commanded urgently, as over the ridge the sound of small-arms fire grew ever louder. 'Don't frigging sit there admiring the view. Gimme a bomb. I'm gonna drop three juicy metal eggs right on them frigging Amis.'

Hastily, he dropped to one knee next to the tube and adjusted the sights. Matz needed no further urging from the huge NCO. He knew that every second counted now if they were going to get the rest of Wotan out of the trap in which they now found themselves. *'In!'* he cried out loud as he dropped the first winged bomb into the tube with a hollow clang.

*'Fire!'* Schulze yelled as Matz turned his head to one side to avoid the full impact of the blast.

There was a hollow twang. A puff of smoke. Blast slammed backwards. Matz felt the dirty ragged uniform tunic whipped against his emaciated body, and the mortar bomb was winging its way into the snow-filled sky, as if it would never stop again.

Suddenly, the whine changed into an obscene howl. Against the white backdrop of the snowstorm, they caught a glimpse of a dark object hurtling down at a tremendous rate.

*Thunk!*

Next instant, the earth beneath their feet trembled violently like a live thing. Screams rang out. Smoke surged upwards in a black mushroom. A moment later it was suffused by a flash of cherry-red flame, and Matz yelled as he dropped yet another deadly bomb into the tube, *'In!'*

*'Fire!'* The next bomb came roaring out of the sky with an obscene, death-bringing howl.

'*Thank God for Schulze and Matz!*' von Dodenburg gasped fervently as he led the survivors down the steep wooded slope that led to the River Sauer far below. Here and there men – uniforms suddenly red with their own blood – were hobbling after him, clinging to their comrades, crying, crazed with pain and the madness of combat, 'Give 'em stick, lads ... Give the Amis stick!' And behind them lay those, sprawled out in violent, unnatural contortions, who would never cry out again.

An Ami loomed out of the trees, his shape wavering and distorted by the snowstorm. He had a machine pistol tucked tightly to his right hip. 'Eat dirt, you Kraut bastard!' he snarled, finger whitening on the trigger.

But von Dodenburg was quicker on the draw. It was the American who *ate dirt*. Von Dodenburg's machine pistol chattered violently. The Ami was flung off his feet as if propelled backwards by a blow from a gigantic fist. A series of blood-red button-holes appeared as if by magic along his broad chest. Next moment he died, choking and drowning in his own blood.

They ran on, followed by the chatter of angry machine-gun fire and the solid thump of Schulze's mortar. Now they were crowding the narrow strip of tree-free bank on the enemy side of the River Sauer. On the German bank there was no sign of life. Von

Dodenburg knew that up on the heights there were the camouflaged bunkers of the Siegfried Line. But they were well hidden, and again there was no response coming from them, even as the pursuing fire of the Amis grew louder and louder. *'Bastards!'* von Dodenburg cursed as he stumbled to a stop, heart beating crazily as if it might well burst out of his rib-cage at any moment due to the strain.

For what seemed a long moment he stood there swaying, staring blank-eyed at the river through the flying snow as if he were unable to think, which was true. His body seemed to be drained of energy as if someone had opened a tap. He really didn't know what to do next.

A burst of fire, running through the snow with little white spurts and ending just before it reached him, awakened him to his danger, and to that of his stalled command. He awoke like a man coming out of a bad dream. He cupped his hands about his mouth and started yelling out orders to his old hares. They needed no urging. They knew now it was nip-and-tuck. The next few minutes would decide whether they lived or died. Without hesitation they waded into the water, trying to keep their balance on the smooth stones below the surface as the fierce current snatched at their feet. They pulled out their belts and flung the ends to each other. With frozen, painful fingers they started to make a makeshift rope.

'*Gott mit uns!*' von Dodenburg said scornfully, thinking of the motto on the German Army belt. He hoped to goddam hell He was right now. Otherwise it would be curtains for what was left of his Wotan. He pulled out the ugly, bulbous flare pistol. He thrust home the big cartridge. In one and the same movement he pointed the pistol above his head and fired.

A red flare exploded above him. It hung there, hissing and sizzling, casting a blood-red hue on the snow. He reloaded and fired once again. This time the flare exploded into a sickly green colour.

With a look of almost desperate longing von Dodenburg stared at the wooded heights beyond, which concealed, he knew, the bunkers and pillboxes of Hitler's famed Westwall, which had held up the enemy ever since the previous September. Why weren't the defenders reacting? Why hadn't they opened up with their big guns at the Americans still advancing upon the handful of Wotan troopers crowding the opposite bank of the River Sauer? Were they afraid of a counter-bombardment? Had they been ordered to conserve their ammunition? Did they suspect a trick? Suddenly, with a feeling of total finality that all was now lost, he gave up. There was no alternative. He had to save what was left of his command the best he could. He had no great hopes that he could do that. The Amis held the heights. They had cover. They were – crowded as they were on the narrow bank – sitting frigging ducks!

Still, he had to try. He cupped his hands about his mouth. With the snowflakes whipping his desperate, wind-red face he cried, 'You greenhorns ... use the belts ... Sling your weapons ... and cross ... *Now!*'

Here and there men hesitated. But the old hares allowed no hesitation.

'Come on, you Christmas tree soldiers ... you perverted banana-suckers ... do you want to live for ever, you dogs!' Screaming furiously, kicking and punching those who hesitated, they started to force the younger troopers into the water to begin crossing.

Almost at once the current caught them. They yelled with cold and fright. Here and there men were swept off their feet. Desperately, they tried to hang on to the makeshift rope. Frantically, the old hares – who had done this often enough before – attempted to grab them and raise them to their feet. But, here and there, they were unsuccessful. Screaming in panic, arms flailing wildly, men attempted to fight the current. To no avail. Still screaming, they were carried away, while a frantic von Dodenburg, eyes filled with despair and tears of rage, watched the heights opposite for any sign of movement. But there was none. Up above, the Americans cried in triumph. An officer came running out of the trees, minus a helmet, face crazed with impending victory. *'All right, guys, let's go and get them chicken-shitters!'*

Twenty metres away, Schulze and Matz, still lugging the heavy mortar and the remaining bombs, took in the situation at once, and the fact that their own people on the other side weren't reacting. 'Holy strawsack!' Matz gasped painfully, 'there's a massacre in the making down there.'

'Not if Frau Schulze's handsome son has anything to say about it,' Schulze declared stoutly. 'Bend!'

'What?'

'You heard me, plush ears. *Bend!*'

Matz bent.

Schulze didn't hesitate a second. He threw the heavy tube over Matz's skinny shoulders.

Matz yelled. His knees almost gave way under the weight. He caught himself in time. 'What in three frigging devils' names, are you up to, Schulze?' he choked.

Schulze didn't answer. He hadn't the time. Hastily, he thrust a bomb down the tube. 'Hold steady,' he commanded.

Now Matz guessed what his running mate was up to. He clenched his yellowing teeth, tensed his skinny frame and took the strain. Schulze fired. The tube, unsecured, leaped up and, next moment, slammed down on Matz's shoulders. He yelled with the pain of that tremendous impact. But he kept his position.

Schulze didn't wait to see the effect of his bomb, which had sailed through the flying snow and was now hurtling down on the wooded ridge beyond. Instead, he grabbed one of the three remaining smoke bombs and thrust it down inside the camouflaged steel tube. He fired instantly. Effortlessly, he heaved another smoke bomb inside and fired once more.

Down by the narrow strand, the two bombs struck home. Almost instantly, a thick black smoke started to rise and mingle with the flying snow, while, on the ridge, the firs were snapping like matchwood, snow was slithering down in a mini-avalanche and fire was already breaking out among the resin-heavy trees which concealed the Siegfried Line bunkers.

Still the Amis came on. Now they were more cautious. They were bent low, weapons at the high port, like men advancing against a heavy wind, tensed and ready, as if half-expecting the mortar bombs to fall on them at any moment. But they feared for nothing. Schulze had two bombs left, one high-explosive, one smoke. If he didn't pull it off now, they were lost. There was nothing more that the two old hares could do to rescue their trapped comrades.

'Holy shit!' Matz moaned. 'I'm knackered, Schulzi. I can't...'

'Just two more rounds,' Schulze cut him off urgently. *'Two!'*

Without waiting to see if Matz was going to buckle under the strain, he threw that last high explosive bomb down the tube. It rattled to the bottom. He hardly waited for it to do so. Next moment he pulled the lever. The tube shivered mightily. It almost fell from Matz's skinny back. Somehow the little man – his wizened face contorted with the agony of it all – held the mortar, and the bomb went sailing over the river to strike home on the German side. The smoke bomb followed. Later Schulze would often say, 'I nearly pissed m'sen waiting for those apeturds to respond!' to which Matz invariably snorted, *'Nearly?* Christ on a crutch, I pissed all the way down my left leg!'

Then it happened. On the heights on the German side there was a tremendous roar. Huge guns belched flame and smoke. The air was torn apart like the sound of a massive piece of canvas being ripped. Like a midnight express racing full speed through an empty station, the twin shells landed right in the middle of the advancing

Americans. Suddenly they were galvanised by frantic electric energy like a bunch of puppets in the hands of a puppet-master who had abruptly gone mad. They shrieked. They danced. Arms and legs flew on all sides in a blood-red explosion. Trees were uprooted. Great gouts of earth shot upwards. In an instant all was noise, confusion, terror and sudden, violent death.

Five minutes later, what was left of Wotan was crawling up the other bank of the River Sauer, followed only by a few desultory shots from the Amis, while the unseen gunners of the Siegfried Line bunkers, roused and angered by having their concrete shelters blasted, fired volley after volley of covering fire.

SS Assault Regiment Wotan had been saved once again, and the fate of Major Glenn Miller, USAAF, had been sealed.

# Junglinster, Luxembourg
# November 1944

# One

Kuno von Dodenburg shook his head. He winced and wished he hadn't. The room came into focus, but his vision was still blurred. No wonder. The night before, he and the survivors had been regaled with as much firewater, suds and champers as they had cared to drink. Then there'd been the girls, whores for the most part, Italian girls who had been brought from what was left of Mussolini's ruined republic in that country to service his renegades fighting reluctantly on the side of the Germans.

Slowly, carefully, he let his gaze wander around the farmer's bedroom, white now with the glare of the sunlit snowscape outside. The girl's clothes were everywhere. Knickers screwed up in a tight ball, as if she hadn't been able to get them off quickly enough. A bra huddled together with an empty bottle of champagne. A sweater spreadeagled at the end of the vanished farmer's wooden bed next to the crucifix, the arms thrust out like a headless swimmer.

243

He turned, stiffly but a little happily like men do when they are pleased with their own prowess in bed and their ability to make their woman squeak, squirm and scream with pleasure. It made a man feel like a man. She was still sleeping, snoring very slightly, face down on the rumpled, stained sheet, and, despite the cold, with the feather bed thrown back to reveal her body: the plump curve of her breasts with their big brown nipples, the rise of her buttocks, the black pubic puff of the source of all delight between her spread legs.

But as he turned the old wooden bed squeaked. The girl started. She opened her dark eyes and saw him. For a moment she obviously couldn't take in who he was. Then she smiled, one of those loving, unqualified, Italian female smiles. *'Cara mia,'* she breathed, and flung open her arms for him to kiss her, as if she were a young bride madly in love with the man who had taken her innocence.

For once Von Dodenburg relaxed. He kissed her, ordering himself not to hear the hard, harsh sound outside of a military encampment coming to life for another day at war. *'Buono ... buono,'* she breathed fervently, as if she were really enjoying herself and not performing for money like the whore she was. *'Molto buono!'* She pressed herself against him and he felt that damp exciting sensation of a naked woman's breasts squashed against his hard bony chest.

For a moment Kuno was happy. It was like in his youth, that old excited sensation at the snow and the presents to come, the promise of new food and surprises; plus the delights of woman and those wonderful secrets she possessed. Then she said, '*You fuck?*'

The illusion vanished.

Kuno pulled himself back, aware even more now of the military sounds and commands coming from outside, emphasising the urgency of the day. He put his feet on the cold floor and started pulling on his trousers. Behind him the Italian girl lit a cigarette and puffed in silence, staring at nothing.

Not far away, Sergeant Schulze was not concerned with such emotions. As he always maintained when in his cups in the sergeants' mess among his cronies, 'I believe in the four *F*s, comrades, find 'em, feel 'em, fuck 'em...' and then would come the punchline, accompanied by a burst of beery laughter, '*forget 'em!*' Now, before he was about to leave the plump nubile blonde – who was no blonde, by the way, as he had soon noticed once she had removed her knickers – and forget her, he was determined to enjoy some of the other precepts.

Sometime in the middle of the night, 'drunk as a field howitzer', as he would have it, he had howled drunkenly at the cold winter moon, 'I'm impotent, damned impotent. I've only been able to shaft her five times this night.' His voice had broken into a sob until her cunning fingers had proved that his drunken diagnosis had been wrong.

Now he was finding that perhaps his prognosis had not been altogether incorrect. He yelled through the open door at a naked Matz who was riding an enormous whore, equally naked, 'Holy strawsack, Matzi, this is taking it out of me!' To which Matz had replied unfeelingly, 'So far she ain't seen much of the taking out!' indicating the fat whore under Schulze, who was smoking a fat cigar, occasionally reaching over to take a bite of the ration chocolate he had brought with him. Schulze, for his part, was jumping up and down on that massive body, gasping frantically, the sweat streaming from his back as if he were trying to pump her full of gas with the pump he had stuck in her. Occasionally, the whore would say, mouth full of chocolate, *'Basta* ... come, come, *Sargento!'* And he would choke, 'What the hell d' yer think I'm frigging well trying to do ... jump off a cliff or something?'

In the event, all good things had to come to an end and Sergeant Schulze, Mrs Schulze's handsome son, neither came nor jumped off a cliff. For outside, the whistles were already shrilling and officers were going from door to door, kicking them so that they shook, crying, 'All Wotan personnel ... Outside ... All Wotan personnel outside for briefing!'

So it was that the half a company or so who were fit and had recovered from that long ordeal of the withdrawal from Aachen were assembled in the great barn of the farmhouse HQ – which smelled of male sweat, animal droppings and human misery – for the secret briefing. They were all hung-over, sapped of strength and uninterested in the usual guff which was given out on such affairs, that is until the officer commanding this section of the Westwall, a brigadier general no less – with his chest covered with tin and even the Knight's Cross of the Iron Cross hanging from his tight collar – snapped, 'I'm going to hand you over to another officer. Now listen, you SS, I know you don't take us army men seriously. Well, you'd better now. For we're no longer in charge. It's your own kind who are taking over now, and you know what will happen to you if you fuck them about.' He touched his hand to the shining peak of his cap and departed without another glance or further word, leaving Schulze to remark, 'Well, for a hairy-assed stubble-hopper of the Wehrmacht, *he* certainly seemed to talk our lingo

... laid it on the line!'

'For a general,' Matz corrected him.

'Naturally ... for a general.'

Obergruppenführer Müller appeared without song or sound, as the Germans put it. One minute he wasn't there, the next he was. He simply strode in from the back door of the barn where the pigs lived and the privies were situated. He was alone and without the usual coterie of elegant adjutants that such people usually collected and kept around them permanently. But in the background a skinny figure in civilian clothes hovered, wringing bony hands. It was his secretary, Heinz, though none of the Wotan men, of course, knew that. Neither were they interested. Their attention was centred on this senior SS general who had appeared so surprisingly in their midst.

As usual, Müller was low-key. '*Morgen, Kameraden,*' he murmured softly, and then without any preamble he commenced. 'You are now sealed off in here. There is a good reason for that. What I have to say to you is highly secret and must remain so. The penalty for not complying is death.' He said the word without emphasis, as if it were simply a fact of life.

Matz leaned over to Schulze, who was picking his nose and gazing at his findings with an air of studious, scientific interest. 'I know the bugger,' he whispered. 'Gestapo

248

Müller. He's bad news. He used to be a cop in Munich when I was a nipper. Hated the Nazis like poison. Now he's one of their big shots. Wouldn't like to get on the wrong side of that bugger!' He looked at the little man with the curiously shaven head and pudding face, as if he were seeing him for the first time.

Schulze sniffed and flipped away another of his excavations. 'Don't wet yersen,' he commented calmly. 'I'll look after yer ... after all, I'm used to you barnshitters from Bavaria.'

'From here,' Müller was saying, while behind him Heinz was scribbling furiously into his notebooks, 'you will be taken to a special camp just near the Cat's Head on the old border with Luxembourg.'

Von Dodenburg frowned, puzzled. The Cat's Head was a seven-storey Siegfried Line bunker, the biggest in this whole section of the line. Did this mean they were going to do some kind of garrison duty while they were reinforced and refitted? Somehow he didn't think so. Why this secrecy, otherwise?

Next moment Gestapo Müller confirmed his thoughts. He said, 'You will spend seventy-two hours there. During that time you will be reinforced, re-equipped and briefed.' He let his words sink in. 'Then you will be dispatched on a special mission.'

Von Dodenburg started. *Not another!* an angry little voice at the back of his mind blurted out. Why always Wotan? Around him the survivors of the break-out from Aachen muttered angrily. They were obviously thinking the same. *Why us?*

'Obergruppenführer,' von Dodenburg began, 'I should like to make a formal protest.'

Müller gave him short shrift. 'You may protest as long as you like, Obersturmbannführer,' he cut in. 'But in your time and in the privacy of your own quarters. Orders is orders. That's that. You do as you're told.' He smirked. It wasn't a pleasant sight. 'You know the alternative?'

Schulze flushed angrily and raised a fist like a small steam shovel. Hastily, Matz pushed down his old comrade's arm. 'Stow it, Schulze,' he hissed urgently. 'It's no use. The bastard'd have the eggs off'n you as soon as look at you. We can't do nothing.'

Corporal Matz was right. There *was* nothing they could do. One hour later they were heading south-east, bound for the Cat's Head and what was soon to come.

# Two

'So we are ... you ... are going to go ahead with it, sir?' Smith said and, if Major Miller had been there, he would have realised his vague suspicion about Smith's accent had been correct. Now the East Coast accent had vanished to be replaced by a definite English upper-class one.

'Yes,' the man in the trenchcoat replied with the full authority of his exalted State Department rank, 'there is no other way. There are those of us in the US Government who cannot go along with the policies of those New Dealers around Roosevelt. Indeed, we suspect too many of them are downright fools and parlour pinks.'

Outside, another shell from the enormous railway gun located somewhere just over the border had landed in the suburbs of Luxembourg City and the horns of police cars and ambulances were shrilling their warning as they sped to the site of the incident. Idly, Smith told himself that the good solid burghers of Luxembourg must be very surprised now, after four years of harmless occupation, to be subjected to German frightfulness at this very moment of Allied liberation. He sniffed and thought yet again that perhaps it had been wrong to invade and attempt to liberate Occupied Europe in the first place. Most of the supposedly oppressed countries had done quite well out of the Huns. The Allies had only brought misery, terror and destruction with them.

The man in the trenchcoat neither saw the thoughtful look on Smith's face, nor seemed to notice the sudden emergency outside Bradley's headquarters. He continued, 'Anyway, we can't let Washington be run by those fools and that crazy bunch of left-wingers and Hebrews around Wallace and Morgenthau. If we did, we might as well give up on Europe and the future – a future – for a beaten Germany after Hitler.'

'A future for Republican big business!' Smith told himself but, in the best British upper-class fashion, his face revealed nothing of his thoughts. It wasn't that he disliked Americans. Indeed he admired many of them and their naive belief that they were the only possessors of vigour and energy in the whole world, that vaunted *get up and go* of theirs about which they were always waffling on. No, it was the fact that they felt Europeans were naive simpletons who were failing to realise, for some unfathomable reason, that the future belonged to the US, which of course it did.

'So,' the man in the trenchcoat said, 'we agree that everything is prepared? The body is kosher? The ID, too, and the bandleader guy, Miller, he'll play along, and you can leave Bradley to me. He'll do everything that Ike orders, and Eisenhower is in our pocket now. He knows which way his bread is buttered if he's going to go into business as you know what...' he flashed a quizzical look at Smith, as if he wondered if he had told the Englishman too much already.

Smith gave him a reassuring, polite smile. As Churchill's representative, he knew that the Great Man supported the daring plan, but that his boss was being very careful in keeping in the background. If anything went wrong, Churchill's policy seemed to be to let the Yanks carry the can. The main thing was to get rid of Hitler and sign an immediate peace before Germany was totally ruined. Then Britain would be faced with holding the whole damned continent together, and Churchill knew he could hardly do that; the Empire's resources were stretched to breaking point as it was.

'Yes, I think we've done all we can at this stage,' Smith reassured the American. 'All we need to know now is when to stage the business from Junglinster.' He allowed himself a little joke, though he knew important

Americans didn't indulge in jokes. They didn't subscribe to old Oscar Wilde's axiom – well, they wouldn't, would they, given Oscar's sexual tastes? – *life is too serious to be taken seriously.* 'In essence, sir, when is Major Miller going to get into his ... er ... *choo-choo* and depart from track fifty-nine?'

Predictably, the man in the trenchcoat was not amused. 'If he knows what's good for him, Major Miller will do exactly as he is told,' he said primly. Outside, another great shell slammed into the ground. The old hotel which had become Bradley's HQ shuddered, and somewhere a glass – or perhaps a picture – tumbled down with a crash. The dust of decades was forced out of the cracks and came down in a thin, grey rain. As someone outside started screaming, '*Medic ... medic ... Oh, mother of God ... my leg ... Medic!*' the man in the trenchcoat said, 'Wonder why the Krauts are beginning to blast now after three months of relative peace. I thought they called this the *Ghost Front* where nothing happens.'

Smith shrugged. 'Search me, sir,' he answered a little irreverently. Then he added, 'Perhaps the Jerries suspect something. I doubt it, but they just might. So I suggest we get this business over with as soon as possible. If Bradley will go along with it, I suggest we make the proposal to the good Germans.'

Obviously, irony was wasted on the other man. 'I agree with you entirely. So, fill me in. How do these Jewish chaps broadcast to the Krauts?'

'In the evening, sir.'

'In the evening?'

'Yessir. When the Jerries come off duty and can find a secret place to listen to the Junglinster broadcasts. You must remember, sir, that to be caught listening to our broadcasts could mean that a chap dies a sudden death.'

'I see ... go on.'

'Well, sir, Captain Habe, who's in charge down there, commences his *Information for the Troops* at twenty hundred hours. It's the usual mix of music, dirty sexual lampoons on the Huns' political masters and generals, plus a bit of hard information, minor German victories and the like. This is aimed at convincing the footsloggers that they are listening to an illegal *German* station run by dissidents and deserters from the Wehrmacht who are based somewhere in the Reich. I guess that most of them have tumbled to the fact that it isn't a German station really. But they like our sexual stuff.'

The man in the trenchcoat pulled a face, but didn't interrupt.

'And so they continue to listen. The younger elements in particular. They're sick of marching songs and brass bands. They're keen on *schwing*, as they pronounce it. That's where Miller comes in. He's one of our minor German victories. Our illegals have gotten hold of him. He's agreed to work with them and play his own music with German texts.' Smith smiled. 'Not a very good ploy, but who cares as long as the Jerries buy our plan. Thereafter there'll be no need for *Radio Anni*.'

'Radio Anni?'

'That's the name Captain Habe has given the Junglinster station. He says *Anni* has a homely feel to the average Hun.'

The other man pulled a sour face. 'Doesn't sound right to me. But no matter. So that's the set-up, eh. A bit shaky. But if it works, that's all that matters, eh?'

Smith nodded his agreement. 'Exactly, sir. As naive as the Jerries are, they might just buy it.'

The man in the trenchcoat stood up. He wasn't a nice man, Smith thought. He guessed he was the kind of American who would become more and more common after the USA had beaten the Germans. In time, people everywhere would think exactly that. It had been an American war. The British had been involved in some minor capacity – perhaps letting the Americans use their island as a kind of launching pad for American fighting troops on their way to liberate Europe – while they, the

British, stayed at home in their cold miserable climate boiling stinking Brussel sprouts and – naturally – drinking tea. 'You're on your way, sir?'

'Yes, it's imperative now that I see Dulles in Berne to take this thing a stage further.'

'I see, sir. Politics?'

'Something like that,' the other man agreed. 'Just see you keep an eye on Miller. You know these cheap musicians ... they're weak sisters at the best of times. Keep him in line.'

'I will, sir,' Smith assured him and stretched out his hand. The man in the trenchcoat didn't seem to notice the gesture. Perhaps his mind was on other things. 'One thing before I go.'

'Sir?'

'If anything goes wrong ... which of course it won't.'

'Naturally, sir.'

Again irony was wasted on the man in the trenchcoat. 'I want you *personally*,' he looked almost fiercely at the Briton, 'to ensure that nothing ever comes out to the general public. You must be responsible for seeing that every last piece of dirt is swept under the carpet. You, after all, are Prime Minister Churchill's representative in this grave and top-secret matter.' Now the American sounded very much like the senior banker turned diplomat which he now was, a man who – in his time – had frightened a lot of people and would, in Smith's opinion, do so a lot more in the future.

'Of course ... I understand, sir,' Smith responded dutifully.

The American lowered his voice. 'May I say this just between the two of us?'

'Sir?'

'In case of failure, it would be better that those in the know should be rendered speechless.' His gaze suddenly bored into Smith's.

Smith staggered back a pace as if he had just been struck physically across the face. 'You mean...' he stuttered ... 'have them ... killed?'

The man in the trenchcoat pulled up his collar in preparation to brave the snow, which had commenced falling outside once more. '*An omelette*, and all that, you know. In these great affairs of state, what does the mere mortal matter?' He touched his fingers to his hat, as if in some kind of military salute. 'Good-bye, and do a job that will make that old boss of yours happy.' And with that he was gone.

Smith had risen. Now he sank back into the old armchair, padded at the back with old copies of the Luxembourger Wort, the capital's newspaper. Although he knew he shouldn't be after what he had gone through in this war so far, he was shocked. The

American had been so cold-blooded about it. *Rendered speechless.* My God, what a way to put it!

Outside, another German shell slammed down, and through the flying snow he could see the great plume of black smoke rising to the east. But he didn't seem to be able to take the sight in. His gaze remained blank. It was like his mind. He simply couldn't seem to get it to function. What was he going to do?

He sat there a long time, as it seemed to him, though in fact it was only a matter of minutes. It was the sudden appearance of Major Miller which finally shocked him out of his reverie.

The bandleader staggered past the MPs at the entrance of the HQ, not appearing even to notice their salutes. His hat was missing and his overcoat torn. His broad, homely face was white and dirty and there appeared to be a crack in the glasses he wore. Smith took all this in in the same moment that he noted that the musician was holding his right hand in front of him like a blind man does when he attempts to find his way in a strange place.

Smith sprang to his feet. 'Glenn!' he called urgently. 'Major Miller!'

Miller turned his head in the direction of the speaker very slowly, as if it was worked by rusty, stiff springs. 'Smith,' he croaked. 'I think I've been hit.' He staggered and, for one horrible moment, Smith thought he might fall down there and then in the middle of the entrance.

Hastily, he rushed towards him, caught Miller by the arm and guided him to the nearest chair and let him fall, noting as he did so that Miller didn't smell of booze as he had first thought, but of smoke: wood smoke. 'You were caught in the shelling?' he prompted, assuming his East Coast accent once more.

Numbly, Miller nodded, as if he were too shocked to be able to speak.

Smith grabbed for his hip-flask, unscrewed the cap and offered it to the bandleader. 'Take a drink of that, Glenn,' he urged. 'That'll put you right. Come on, down the hatch now. You need it by golly!'

Miller did as he was told, coughing and spluttering as he did so. But the colour returned to his cheeks and his eyes behind the cracked spectacles focused correctly once more. 'Thanks,' he gasped. 'You were right ... I needed that.'

Smith took the flask from him. But he didn't put it back in his pocket, just in case. Miller's fingers were still trembling, and now for the first time he noticed the thin trickle of bright red blood running down the side of Miller's pale face. 'You've been hit!'

Miller shook his head. 'Not much. Just a

scratch. I won't get the Purple Heart for it, that's for sure.'

'Many men have for less, Glenn, you know.'

'No, the guys would think I was gold-bricking, but Jesus, I sure would have liked that million dollar wound the GIs talk about.'

'The one that gets them sent back to the States, Glenn?'

'Yeah.' Miller fumbled inside his pocket and finally found a handkerchief to wipe away the blood, which was becoming a nuisance.

Abruptly, Smith felt very sorry for the musician. He was forty, too old for this sort of thing, he told himself, and totally out of his depth in a combat zone. 'I guess you'd like to go home, Glenn,' he said softly.

Miller wearily looked at his blood-stained handkerchief and nodded his head. 'Yeah, I'd give my right arm to be back home now, just in time for Christmas. I made a big mistake. I'm just not cut out for this sort of thing. I just want to get on with my old life, wife, kids, new house, the band and a round of golf now and again, if I can squeeze it into the schedule.' He sighed and started to speak, then changed his mind and fell silent somewhat sadly.

'Listen, Glenn, you carry out what the big shots want you to do here and I'll push for you to be sent home, say on medical grounds. Everyone knows you tried your damndest to get into the service although you were well over draft age and were married with kids. You've done your duty and people know that. They know you're not chickening out now. There'd be no stigma about your returning home.'

Miller looked at him, new hope in his lacklustre eyes. 'You mean that? You'd help?'

'Sure I would,' Smith said with more enthusiasm than he felt. 'I haven't got much personal clout, but the people I work with have. They tell the military what to do and they pop to and do it, or else!'

'Gee, that would be swell!' Miller enthused, like one of those newfangled teenagers, Smith couldn't help thinking, using the new word from the other side of the Atlantic. 'But what about Ike? ... I got the impression from talking to him that whatever I'm supposed to do is top secret. Almost as if the big shots are not going to let me go that soon, even when this, er, mission is over.' He looked at Smith. 'And what is the mission really ... I mean, what has my music got to do with that stiff we hauled back here from that awful burial place in Belgium? Those poor guys.' He hung his head suddenly.

Smith clapped him hastily on the shoulder. He didn't want Miller to go back into shock. That would be fatal. His nerves were so strung out by the shell incident and the way that the Brass had pressured him over the last weeks that the old bandleader might well go into a kind of permanent shock. After all, he didn't have the resilience of the average combat GI half his age. 'Listen, Glenn,' he said, lowering his voice so that none of the passing officers on Bradley's staff could hear. 'I'm going to tell you as much as I dare about what the Brass expects you to do. But you must promise me that you'll tell no one that I have told you. It would be more than my job's worth. There could be very serious effects on my health.' He didn't specify what, but Miller looked shocked, as if he was realising for the first time that he was involved in something that was highly dangerous, and not only to the enemy. 'I promise you. I won't breathe a word.'

'I know you wouldn't, Glenn.' Smith took a deep breath, like someone prepared to spring off a high-diving board into deep water. 'In the old war,' Smith commenced, cleared his throat and then began again for some reason known only to himself. 'In the First World War the Germans and the French fought a protracted battle for a French town not so far from here, named Verdun.'

'I've heard of it.'

'Well, both sides took hundreds of

263

thousands of casualties between 1916 and nearly to the end of the war when the battle ended. For French and Germans the key to success was the capture of the forts the French had built there at the end of the 19th century. Every time one of them was captured and recaptured it was hailed by the press of both sides as a major success. But mostly, especially on the German side, the heroes of the fortress battles were officers. Noncoms and ordinary soldiers might do the hard fighting, but it was their officers who got the medals, even if they didn't do much to achieve victory. It was the class and caste system of that time.'

'Kinda like the Limeys today,' Miller suggested.

Smith smiled inwardly. 'Yes, something like that. Anyway, there was one German NCO who they couldn't refuse to honour because in 1917, he captured one of the forts that had previously cost 10,000 German lives in an abortive attack. The man was promoted to sergeant major and later, when the Imperial German Army was becoming bolshy, the Kaiser decided to award him the country's highest honour to encourage the rank and file to keep on fighting. I think our man was the only enlisted man in the German Army to receive the Pour le Mérite, the equivalent of our Congressional Medal. The man – named

Hausmann by the way – became a national hero. Even more so after the war when he refused to let his name be used by the socialists for their political ends. He said simply, "I'm going on to my old job, which was driving a team for a brewery." '

Glenn looked puzzled but said nothing, something for which Smith was glad. He was thinking furiously as he related his tale of the past, wondering just how much he could safely tell Miller. Outside, another of the great shells slammed into the city. But neither seemed to notice it this time. They were both engrossed in the story.

'When Hitler took over in 1933 he naturally wanted to recruit Hausmann to his Workers' Party. Hausmann would have none of it, although the Nazis offered him great honours. He maintained to the Press, "I'm just a driver for a brewery. I know nothing about politics. Here is where I stay." And that was that.'

'Surprisingly enough,' Smith continued, 'in 1939 when Germany went to war he volunteered for infantry. Why, we don't know. Patriotism perhaps. Possibly he'd had enough. He just wanted to get it over with and die in battle. But, if that was the reason, he didn't manage it. Fate was against him. He survived till the German defeat at Stalingrad in 1942 then, after three years of war, he spoke out against Hitler's murderous regime. Naturally, the Nazis wanted to shut him up. If he'd have been just some ordinary Joe, they would have quietly got rid of him.' He put his two fingers to his temple and made a gesture with them, as if he were pulling the trigger of a pistol. 'But he wasn't. He was a popular hero, especially among the rank and file of the German Army. Instead he was posted to a punishment battalion as a quick way of getting rid of him at the front...'

'Punishment battalion?' Miller enquired, dabbing the blood from his face.

'Yes. The Germans have two of them: the 666th and the 999th. They're sent out to clear away minefields, attack bunkers etc ... suicide missions and the like.'

'I see.'

'But Hausmann's luck held out when all around, it seems, his fellow soldier-prisoners were dying like flies. Indeed, he survived the campaign in France till September, when he was finally hit and captured by our 1st Army. He fell into the hands of a decidedly smart interrogation team. They tumbled to who he was, especially as the German High Command put out a special bulletin with all the usual bombastic bullshit they use on such occasions. The Krauts thought Hausmann was dead and they could safely maintain that he had been a great hero who had volunteered for the infantry as a simple soldier when he was well over age.' He looked at Miller and realised that Hausmann was only a couple of years older than the American bandleader, but what a different life-style the two of them had led!

Outside, the sirens – high above the gabled eighteenth-century roofs of the old city next to the twin spires of the Notre Dame cathedral – were beginning to sound the all clear. The bombardment had ceased for a while. Smith forced a smile. 'The Krauts are going to take a coffee break, Glenn,' he said, attempting to cheer the bandleader up.

But Miller's pale face remained somber. 'Go on,' he urged, as if he realised that this long account of the German war hero had something to do with himself.

'What the German High Command didn't know, Glenn, was that Karl Hausmann had not been killed in combat. In fact, he was recovering in the US General Field Hospital in Liège and – this is the important thing – Hausmann was prepared to talk at last. He'd had enough. As soon as he was fit enough he was going to go...'

'On the radio and spill the beans,' Miller interrupted.

'Yeah, that had been the plan.'

'*Had?*'

'Yes.' Smith pulled a face. 'The poor fellow died on us. That's why we had that journey to the obscure pathologist out in Belgium where all the stiffs were. We wanted to be completely sure that Hausmann's corpse would reveal nothing to the enemy.'

Miller looked completely puzzled now. 'You've lost me,' he stuttered. 'My head's spinning. I don't know where I am.'

Smith gave him a faint sympathetic smile. 'We in Intelligence are notorious for favouring an oblique approach. A *very* oblique one. We wanted an expert opinion far from headquarters and hospitals. Doctors and staff officers are like old women, noted for their damned tittle-tattle. Our pathologist's only choice of conversational partner would be his stiffs and those poor, unfortunate coloured chaps who did all the hard work. He was safe for us.'

'But why all the secrecy, and what do you intend to do with this Kraut stiff?'

'Give him back to the Krauts,' Smith said simply.

'Give him back to the Krauts!' Glenn Miller exclaimed, coming to life for the first time since he had been knocked almost senseless by the explosion of the German shell. 'What the Sam Hill do you mean by that?'

But before Smith had a chance to answer a firm but pleasant voice said, 'General Bradley will see both of you now. He's giving you ten minutes.'

# Three

'First company ready, sir!' Schulze yelled, as if he were back on the parade ground of the *Leibstandarte* in Berlin, his breath fogging a thick grey cloud on icy mountain air.

'Second company ready, sir!' Matz tried to outdo his running mate, though he felt they were both arsing around. For the first company consisted of exactly thirty men and his own of twenty: fifty old hares and greenhorns in all, the size of two platoons.

But Obersturmbannführer Kuno von Dodenburg responded as if these were the victorious old days and he was commanding two full companies of three hundred men or more. He felt the greenhorns straight from the depot, going into action for the first time, deserved to feel that this was something more important than just a raid. He raised his right hand to the cracked peak of his battered hat, adorned with the tarnished skull and crossbones of the SS, and cried back smartly, '*Erste and Zweite Kompanien ... wegtreten!*'

The two old hares went along with the

stupid game. As one they roared back, *'Danke, Obersturmbannführer!'* Then, swinging round in the snow in perfect unison, they commanded, *'Achtung ... Stillgestanden ... Wegtreten!'* Smartly, the handful of troopers marched away through the new snow, heading for the little column of white-painted half-tracks straight from the factory, engines already running, the drivers gunning them so that the vehicles quivered like thoroughbred horses anxious to be given their head.

Müller, muffled in a thick general's great-coat complete with fur collar and huge fur mittens, nodded his approval. 'They'll do it, Obersturm. They're the best the Fatherland can provide this winter. They're keen.'

Von Dodenburg wasn't convinced, but he kept his reservations to himself. Instead, he said, 'I would appreciate it, sir, if you could arrange for another allocation of shells, say fifty per gun, to the Cat's Head. The heavier and more prolonged the barrage is, the more chance we have to get within striking range of Junglinster by dawn. If we lose too many men before we attack...' He shrugged and didn't complete his sentence.

'Take it as done, von Dodenburg', Müller said. 'We're all aware of the importance of this mission. You have priority. The Führer himself has ordered that.'

'Thank you.'

Müller put out his hand. Von Dodenburg ignored it. He didn't like the Bavarian. He was one of those who had fought the war behind a desk, sending others to their deaths, young men who had not even begun to live yet. Müller and his sort would probably die in bed of old age if they were lucky. Instead, he raised his threadbare grey glove to his cap and snapped, *'Bitte um mich abzumelden, Obergruppenführer?'*

Müller touched his cap casually. He had been a sergeant in the last war. He didn't hold with all this saluting and clicking of heels and the like. It smacked too much of the *sow Prussians* that every right-thinking Bavarian detested. 'You know the stakes, von Dodenburg. This is our last chance to root out the traitors and defeatists who are undermining our Homeland. You mustn't fail.'

'I won't, Obergruppenführer,' said von Dodenburg, his mind full of what Müller had told him the night before. But he also thought of those greenhorns now pushing and shoving excitedly to clamber into the waiting half-tracks like a bunch of happy schoolkids eager to be off and away from the classroom on some summer excursion. He had to save those youths. They were Germany's future. They were the ones that really counted.

*'Gut. Dann Hals und Beinbruch,'* Müller

wished. *Happy landings.*

'Thank you, sir.' Von Dodenburg turned and then he was sprinting lightly through the snow to where the little convoy waited. Müller watched him go. There was a little admiration in his gaze. Von Dodenburg was the best of officers, keen, fit; not one of those titled swine who sacrificed their men in order to gain honours for themselves. All the same, he was still one of those aristocratic *Monokelfritzen* who had to be eradicated if Moscow ever wanted to control the Germans after the defeat.

For one more minute he watched the SS clustering around their vehicles on the snowy track below, and thought of Hausmann and the Amis' foolish propaganda ploy, and the fact that they had played right into his hands in this unexpected manner. Then he dismissed the lot of them. They were already history. He strode back to where Heinz, wringing his bony hands as usual, was waiting by the car.

'Well, as I was saying,' Schulze yelled above the rattle of the tracks as the armoured fighting vehicle ploughed its way down the rough farm road that led out of the hills towards the shattered little border town of Irrel. 'Never let yersen fall into the hands of the pox doctors if you can help it. They're worse than the frigging Popovs. The last run-in I had with 'em, just before we got

272

run out of Paris, there were half a dozen of the dirty-minded swine playing with my tail. Professor Doctor this ... Doctor-Doctor that. They had a hold on my love-stick as if they might pull it off at any moment. Really put the shits up Frau Schulze's handsome son, I can tell yer!'

'Well, what was wrong with yer, Sarge?' one of the open-mouthed greenhorns listening asked.

'Put a *sergeant* on that, arse-without-ears!' Schulze snapped and then, all sweetness and light once more, he continued, 'Well, sonny, when grown men go to bed with the ladies to dance the mattress polka, they sometimes take away with them a little souvenir, which isn't too nice of the ladies to give them.' He beamed at the smooth-faced youngster.

Von Dodenburg smiled in spite of his worries and inner tension at what was to come. They had perhaps only a fifty-fifty chance of coming back once the Amis were alerted to their presence behind their lines.

The greenhorn went on, 'I'd have thought you'd have been glad of a present after your dance. It's usually the other way around, isn't it, Sergeant?'

Schulze looked at the boy pityingly and then appealed to Matz with what appeared to be a throb in his throat. 'Can you frigging well believe it, Matzi!' he exclaimed. 'What kind of frigging cannon-fodder are they sending us from the depot these days!' He shook his head in mock wonder and continued with his long, winding tale as the little convoy wound its way ever closer to the ruined bridge across the River Sauer where they would sneak across into Luxembourg and on to the surprise raid. 'Then it got worse. They asked me to bend down. Being the tame obedient feller that I am, I obliged in all my innocence and do you know what those perverted warm brothers o' so-called doctors did then?'

'No,' the greenhorns cried, falling for it, while Matz clasped his head as if he had been attacked by a massive migraine.

'One of 'em stuck his finger right up my arse!' He shuddered dramatically, as if he were still outraged at that dastardly assault on his manhood. 'I mean, I know that medics can be warm brothers like everybody else, including most of you greenhorns. I know you've all got tins o' vaseline hidden in yer knapsacks. But I didn't think they'd do it so openly. I thought it was agin that oath they swore, hypocrites oath or something, named after some old Greek pervert, I believe...'

Von Dodenburg let Schulze's voice recede into the background as he started to consider Müller's briefing once more, realising as he did so just how important this mission seemed to the Party *Prominenz*. After all, it wasn't every day that a broken-down commander of a depleted regiment of the Armed SS was briefed by the head of the Gestapo, and a Police and SS General to boot.

'Now, we've known about this damnfool, so-called clandestine radio station of theirs – this *Radio Anni* – for weeks,' Müller had sneered. 'Do they think we of the Gestapo don't posses radio location units to pinpoint such outfits? Why, we've been using them to trace clandestine stations since the Führer came to power in '33. And Junglinster isn't on the other side of the shitty moon, is it?'

Von Dodenburg had nodded his head and listened without speaking. He didn't quite trust Müller and he didn't like him, that was for certain. So he thought he'd better keep his mouth shut and limit his remarks to questions of military detail if they occurred.

'We know all about those Jews over there, and their American monkey music they feed these gullible stubble-hoppers of ours. We know, too, about the station being employed to maintain links between the Ami politicians and generals and the traitors in our own homeland. You understand, von Dodenburg?'

'Yessir!' he had replied, 'I understand.' He had limited himself to just that. Like so many important people, Müller liked to hear himself speak. Others were just mere sounding boards.

'Now, however, things have come to a head. The station maintained in its last evening broadcast that someone who has a symbolic value for the ordinary German stubble-hopper has died in Ami captivity and is to be returned through them to the German people.' Abruptly, von Dodenburg had become interested and had asked swiftly, 'Who, sir?'

'Have you ever heard of Sergeant Major Hausmann?'

'Why, yessir!' he had answered, surprised. 'As boys we all learned what he did at Verdun. But I've never heard of him for years. But why...'

'Another damned misfit,' Müller interrupted, his broad peasant face contorted with disgust. 'Damned nuisance with all his shitting posturing. Well, to cut a long story short, he's to be handed back to the German authorities, and you know why. The Amis are going to use him as a gesture.'

'What kind of gesture?'

'That they're not fighting the German people, but the people they maintain sent the *Verdun hero*' – he emphasised the words with a sneer – 'to his death. Naturally, those rats who are trying to betray us will use the whole sickening business to call for the end of the National Socialist regime and the removal of the Führer.'

Von Dodenburg had sensed immediately the immense potential of this transfer. The great majority of the German nation were war weary, even the Armed SS. Many only continued fighting because they knew there was no alternative. It was march or croak, as the regimental motto of Wotan had it. Officially, the Allies demanded unconditional surrender. But if the transfer of Hausmann's body brought forward a German opposition who were prepared to treat with the enemy as the failed plotters of the previous July had wanted to do, the Allies might quietly forget that draconian *unconditional surrender*.

Schulze was still on his comic tale of woe at the hands of the *pox doctors* and von Dodenburg realised suddenly that he had been placed in a moral dilemma. Should he help to prolong this murderous war or should he abort his mission and help to bring it to an end?

He looked at the boyish, innocent faces of the greenhorns listening to the old hare and saw in them the future. He and the old hares, like Schulze, Matz and the rest, were the past. Should he save them, or should they all go down with the sinking ship of the Third Reich in the inevitable tragedy to come.

But even as he considered that overwhelming decision the hollow boom of artillery fire, followed an instant later by the screech of shells coming across the border at the little convoy, told him they were in trouble. Decisions had to be postponed. His immediate duty was to save Wotan.

'What a frigging piggery!' Schulze shouted. 'Just when I was giving these wet tails a bit of frigging culture. I'll have...'

'Shut up!' von Dodenburg interrupted him frantically as the enemy shells started to walk their way towards the abruptly-stalled little convoy of half-tracks, guided by some hidden field artillery observer on the other side of the river, *'Vollgas! Nix wie raus!'*

The drivers needed no urging. Like ants disturbed by someone overturning the stone under which they were hidden they scuttled for cover, crashing over the embankment, gears whining under pressure, heading for the pines and a safe hiding place.

# Four

'Jingle bells, jingle bells, jingle all the way. Oh what fun it is to ride on a one-horse, open sleigh,' the MP sergeant sang happily as he and the other American staff of Station Anni – cooks, orderlies, drivers and the like – hurried back and forth preparing the boxes containing the Christmas goodies. Every man in the station high on the hill above Junglinster had sacrificed his candy ration and other supplies – ordinary to him but unbelievable treasures to the civilians – to prepare a Christmas feast for the local kids.

Captain Hans Habe, the station chief, grinned, pleased at the happiness of the Americans and, although he was Jewish and born a German, he felt a little of their happiness and excitement at the approach of Christmas.

Next to him Stefan Heym, another exile who had fled the Nazis to America, said sourly, 'I don't know why you should be so cheerful, Hans. All this American Christmas rubbish doesn't mean a thing to us. You're

279

not even a Christian and, besides, you know as well as I do it's all fake, commercial, pagan trash in order for capitalists to sell cheap rubbish. *Ach*,' he cursed in German, '*es ist doch zum Kotzen!*'

Habe was not offended by his old comrade's outburst. He was used to them. Besides, over Christmas he had a three-day pass to Paris, and a chic, French mademoiselle waiting for him there, too, with the hotel and bath already booked and – hopefully – the champagne on ice. 'Give in a little, Stefan,' he urged, as one of the drivers entered with the red-berried holly he had picked in the woods near the station and was going to hang about the place in the American fashion. 'Relax, as the Yanks say. Enjoy it. It adds a bit of brightness to our grim war-time world.'

'Adds more money to the cash tills in America,' Heym said as sourly as before, not yielding an inch. 'Religion and superstition; opium of the people, mingled with primitive mumbo-jumbo.'

'Listen to this,' Habe interrupted. 'It's from *Pickwick Papers* by the Englishman Dickens.'

'And what a phoney he was,' Heym said.

'*Ach, halt die Schnauze,*' Habe cursed halfheartedly. He was in too good a mood to be really angry. He bent to the text and read slowly in his careful American-English accent: 'How many families, whose members have been dispersed and scattered far and wide in the restless struggle for life, are then reunited in that happy state of companionship and mutual good-will, which is a source of such sure and unalloyed delight. How many recollections and how many dormant sympathies does Christmas time awaken.'

'He was paid at a penny a word. That's why he was so verbose,' Heym mocked. 'If anyone was a humbug, to use his own term, it was Charles Dickens.'

With a sigh, Captain Habe gave up. 'What a miserable old cynic you are, Stefan. For a communist, a man of the common people, you have precious little sympathy with ordinary folk. I swear you have ice-cold water in your veins instead of blood.'

Heym opened his mouth to object, but he didn't manage it. From the entrance to the long corridor flanked with generators and other machines, which ran the length of the station, the MP on guard called, 'The trucks are coming, sir. They'll be at the gate in half a minute.'

'Okay, Al, got it,' Habe said.

Habe turned to Heym, who was pointing at the box-like refrigerator van that brought up the end of the little convoy of olive-drab staff cars, his mouth open to speak. *'Don't,'* he said firmly. 'Don't ask questions! And

281

that's an order, Stefan.' Hurriedly, he added as the first sedan turned off into the snowy drive, 'You know what these Americans think of us Jews who are Germans, speak with a funny accent and wave their arms about a lot. We don't want to confirm them in their racial stereotypes.'

Heym sneered but said nothing.

Habe nodded as if he was satisfied that he had got his message across and tugged at his smart tunic. 'Okay, Heym,' he said formally, in his best American English. 'Let's get on the ball, eh?'

Heym snapped to attention as the Americans did and touched his hand to his forehead. 'Yessir, captain, sir!'

'Fuck you!' Habe said laconically and hurried to the entrance, placing himself at the top of the steps as the two MPs posted there came to attention. The first staff car, containing Smith and Glenn Miller, rolled to a stop. The scene was set, the actors were in place, the drama could now commence.

Von Dodenburg held up his hand, fingers outspread on the top of his helmet. It was the traditional signal for *rally on me*. Like white ghosts his men, all now clad in camouflaged snow suits, slid out of the snow-burdened firs and came closer to crouch to the left and right of their CO.

Down below, the flood plain of the River

Sauer was spread out as if seen from a plane coming in to land. Speaking softly, though there wasn't an Ami, as far as he knew, within half a kilometre of them, von Dodenburg briefed his little force. 'Echternach.' He indicated the little town on the other side of the river, most of its buildings shattered by three months of German counter-fire, though the Basilica was still intact. 'Naturally, there is an Ami garrison; a small one .... Those hotels at two o'clock' – he pointed to the two pre-war tourist hotels, looking worse for wear, just outside the Luxembourg town along the road which ran north – 'also occupied by the enemy. Therefore, we take the left flank. There, there are no Amis.'

'But no cover either, sir!' Schulze objected, looking worried and speaking at just below a roar, which was very unusual for him, a sign that he was troubled.

'It's a chance we'll have to take. Make you keep your big keester down, Schulze,' he added, trying to lighten the tension.

'Most women admire it, sir,' Schulze replied with a grin. 'A lovely arse they say ... *Richtig zum Anbeissen.*'

'Ugh!' Matz pulled a face. 'Disgusting.'

'I think, with a bit of luck and the new snow soon to fall, we'll make it. Then it's into the hills parallel to the minor road which leads to Junglinster. Once in position, it's going to be strike and scoot.'

Schulze said a silent prayer that the CO was going to be right with his *shoot and scoot.*

If von Dodenburg was worried, he didn't show it. His lean, hard face radiated the confidence of the great days of 1940, when Wotan had swept all before it, and those long-dead, blond giants, perfect specimens of Germanic manhood, had become the terror of any front on which they fought. 'I'll take the point,' he ordered. 'You follow, Schulze. Corporal Matz, you'll bring up the rear.'

'As usual!' Matz pretended to grumble to encourage the frightened-looking green-horns. 'I allus am in the fart wind of Schulze's thin shits brigade.'

'Watch I don't blast off...' Schulze began with his insult, but von Dodenburg cut him short, 'Blast off down that slope, Schulze, exactly five minutes after I've gone with the point.' He looked at his watch. 'Now, cir...'

But an irrepressible Schulze beat him to it with the old army quip, 'Circumcise your watches.'

Von Dodenburg grinned and gave in. 'It is now exactly five minutes after...' Then he was off with half a dozen of the greenhorns, slithering down the snowy slope with Matz and Schulze watching, a sudden worried look in their red-rimmed eyes. Above them the sky darkened even more. Slowly, gently, almost imperceptibly, the first soft white flakes started to drift down.

'The drill is this.' Habe was proud of his knowledge of US Army terminology. Now he turned it on full blast at his visitors, while Stefan Heym watched in cynical amusement. 'At zero eight each morning we give them a flash of what is to come on the evening programme. We dose it with scuttlebutt and the usual sort of latrine rumours we get in our own army...'

'Our own army,' Heym told himself. 'What a shit Jew Habe is, fooling himself like this.' It wasn't *his* army, any more than Hitler's Nazi legions were.

'Wet their appetite, sort of.'

Smith nodded while Miller, a patch on his wounded forehead, listened expressionless, as if all this was happening to someone else. He wasn't even interested enough to ask about this remote border radio station's technical facilities. It was all like a dream – a bad one – to him.

'Then at twenty hundred hours we go on the air. We give the Krauts plenty of time to find us on their low-frequency radios. We could do that in the morning, but we don't want their jamming stations to home in on us too soon. Otherwise they'd blast us off the air with their military bands and the like.'

Again Smith nodded as if he were interested, though, of course, he knew all this. Still, the captain was obviously very proud of his operation. He forced himself to fake interest. Outside, it was beginning to snow again. He hoped it would not settle too much. The road back to Luxembourg City after the broadcast tonight would be tough. All up and down hills. His attention wandered as he looked through the as yet unblacked-out windows of the station. Through the white haze he thought he glimpsed a red signal flare. He craned his neck and peered harder. But there was no more red light. Perhaps it had been some nervous GI signalling his Command Post for assistance. Perhaps he hadn't seen anything at all. He turned his attention back to Habe, who was concluding with, 'Well, gentlemen, that's the set-up, and Major Miller...'

'Yes?'

'I take it as a great honour, as do all my men, that you have come here personally. I know that the enemy over the other side of that ridge will appreciate it as well. Their young guys are nuts about swing music, especially yours.'

'Thank you,' Miller said, but his voice held no conviction and suddenly his gaze was fixed on the distant line of hills where the Germans were. Suddenly he realised that this was the real shooting war. Here American soldiers got killed!

Smith took over. Now was the time to get down to the real reason for this night's broadcast. 'You've been informed, Captain,' he snapped, very business-like now, 'of the importance of your announcement this night.'

Habe nodded.

'I want you to take care of it personally. You must read the script exactly as it is printed. There must be no deviation from that text. While you're reading it, and for the rest of the night afterwards, I want your people and those we've brought up with us from General Bradley's Radio Intelligence to be on instant alert – and response – for any message we might receive from over there.' With a nod of his head, he indicted the darkening ridge line where the Germans were. 'There must be no slip-ups,' he ended. 'And instant response. I can assure you that this is vital to the American war effort. You understand?'

'Fully.'

'Good. One last thing, Captain Habe.'

'Sir?'

'Until you are ordered otherwise – and that order may never come – you will keep what transpires here this night totally and utterly secret. Is that understood?' Smith gave Habe a hard look and next to him, a still bemused Miller was sufficiently perceptive, however, to tell himself that Smith, the former schoolteacher, was a very hard man indeed. Suddenly and startlingly, he realised that he had been led up the garden path. Smith, which was naturally not his name at all, had never been a schoolteacher in all his life. He shivered for some reason he couldn't quite explain.

Outside, only barely visible in the increasing snowstorm, the red lights continued to explode above the front. But no one there at that moment noticed. A decisive moment in the secret history of World War Two was passing, but those who were present and would survive didn't even note that passing.

'The swine know we're here,' von Dodenburg told himself grimly, as yet another red flare hissed into the snowy sky perhaps some hundred and fifty metres away. He guessed the Amis sensed there was something wrong but didn't quite know what. As was the case in all armies, the *Nervous Nellies* broke their inner tension by firing flares, letting off a few bursts with their weapons; anything that would relieve the almost unbearable pressure. As if on cue there was a burst of tracer to his right. Red bullets hissed through the snowstorm like a flight of angry hornets. Here and there his greenhorns faltered and flinched. 'Stand fast, boys,' he said cheerfully. 'It's only the fat Amis farting.' It was crude, but in combat everything was basic, brutal, crude. They ploughed on.

By now von Dodenburg estimated they had outflanked the enemy positions at Echternach. Before them was the narrow country road that led to Junglinster and then on to Luxembourg City. He guessed that there might be irregular patrols to left and right of the hill road – after all, Luxembourg City was the headquarters of the US Army Group – but there'd definitely be roadblocks on the road itself. Even the Amis, as careless as they were, could not allow a potentially key road leading from the front to their main HQ to be uncontrolled. Now, von Dodenburg decided, the main danger would be the chance of bumping into one of these roadblocks concealed by the blinding snowstorm.

On the other hand, he considered – as the wind blew the razor-sharp snow particles into his wind-reddened face like the point of a keen stiletto blade – the snowstorm was on their side too. They'd be concealed from prying Ami eyes.

He consulted the green glowing dial of the compass strapped to his right wrist. They were well on course. He'd give it another ten minutes or so at this pace and on this course, then signal the two groups to close up. He wanted to hit that radio station with all the force he had and then, before the balloon went up in Luxembourg City some twenty kilometres away, be on his way with any looted Ami vehicles they could find back to the River Sauer and the Reich. On tricky commando missions like this speed and surprise counted most. Catch the enemy off guard, kick him in the balls and run for it like a devoted coward. He remembered old Vulture's phrase with a faint smile, as if he were recalling a faint passage from some almost forgotten schoolbook. How long ago that seemed; almost another age through which it appeared barely possible one had lived!

He dismissed Vulture and the old, long-vanished Wotan and concentrated on the task in hand. The snowstorm was getting worse. It lashed the tortured faces of the greenhorns – who were not used to weather of this kind – blinding them, filling their lungs with flakes and icy air, stabbing at them so that they gasped for breath as if they were choking. Even the old hares, the veterans of Russia and that country's terrible winters, were finding the going tough. But they soldiered on with grim-faced determination in that manner which was unique to the SS. Looking back at them every now and again – white plodding ghosts barely glimpsed through the howling storm – von Dodenburg felt proud of them and proud to be one of them. No other troops in the world would have been capable of such effort, especially now when Germany had virtually lost the war. Why should these ordinary working men – who had not profited from the last twelve years of the Third Reich like so many of the rear echelon stallions back home in their comfortable, safe HQs – risk their necks in these last days of a war already virtually lost? Why?

A sudden burst of tracer close by made him forget his amateur philosophising on the nature of the fighting man. In a lethal morse code the glowing red slugs zipped across the snowy waste, kicking up little flurries of white about fifty metres away. Von Dodenburg reacted instinctively. God knows, he had done it often enough in the past. *'Volle Deckung!'* he yelled.

His men, greenhorns and old hares alike, needed no urging. They dropped as one, bringing up their weapons and clicking off the safeties in one and the same motion. Even as they hit the deck, their eyes were peering to left and right, and then to their front, trying to penetrate the gloom.

Von Dodenburg was chancing his luck. He had dropped to his right knee. From that position, dangerous as it was, he had a better view. In his right hand he now held the fat bulbous brass signal pistol. It was a dodge he had used more than once with inexperienced enemy troops when they had run into an ambush. All he needed now was for the enemy to show themselves in person or by opening fire once more. Raising his voice, he called in his best English, 'Why the hell are you firing at us? Hey Joe, what's going on?'

It didn't work in the way that some would have expected. As von Dodenburg had half-expected. Instead of an answer in words, they received a swift controlled burst of machine-gun fire. That was another expected reaction and one that von Dodenburg could now use. 'Machine-gunner!' he called, keeping his eye on the spot from which the burst had come. 'Target three o'clock, large bush ... *fire!* Rest ... Ready to move out on my signal.'

In an instant all hell broke loose.

To the rear the two grenadiers carrying the light mortars reacted exactly as von Dodenburg had hoped they would without orders. They dropped to their knees in the snow, stuck a bayonet in front of them to roughly measure the angle and fired. *Thwack!* The small mortar bomb raced into the whirling white sky. Next moment it screeched down again. As von Dodenburg had expected it was not one hundred per cent accurate. But it was close enough. As abruptly as it had started, the machine-gun fire ceased.

'*Los!*' von Dodenburg cried urgently.

The men needed no urging. They surged forward, firing from the hip as they did so. Here and there the Amis rose to meet them. Some fired. Others stood their ground with their bayonets. There was a harsh metallic boom as the two sides clashed. Bayonets and entrenching tools flashed and cleaved. No quarter was given or expected. It was each man for himself. Men swayed back and forth in the driving, blinding snow. Mouthing terrible obscenities, they battled together liked crazed beasts, carried away by that awesome, unreasoning bloodlust of battle. Men fell to the ground wounded and bleeding. It was a fatal fall. The enemy was upon them, slashing, thrusting, gouging. Screams and yells of agony rose on all sides.

Then suddenly, startlingly, as if some hand had opened a concealed tap, the Americans' courage drained away. One moment they were fighting all out, the next they were begging for mercy, praying for succour to a God who looked the other way, throwing away their weapons in unreasoning, absolute panic and fleeing into the snow-white darkness. It was all over. Wotan had broken through. The way to the lonely hilltop radio station was free.

# Five

Smith frowned. He was sure he had heard the typical, brittle, angry snap-and-crackle of a firefight, even though the falling snow, coming down now in a solid white wall, muted every sound. But now it was over. All they could hear was the howl of the wind and the rattle of the big art deco windows, as the snowflakes pelted the glass. He frowned even more. What was he supposed to do? Should he cancel the whole bloody business while there was still time? Or were his nerves playing him up and he was simply imagining the whole thing?

He flashed a look at Miller who was being briefed by Captain Habe. He seemed relaxed for the first time since he had been brought into this strange business. Probably the normalcy of the radio station was having its effect. Now he could concentrate on what he did best, preparing for a concert with his band, albeit on records. He licked his lips, which seemed suddenly parched and very dry. At this moment he would have given his left ball for a stiff drink of scotch, followed by a beer chaser, even *Henri Funck*, the local Luxembourg brew. But he knew there was no time for that. He had to make a decision and if he withdrew Miller now, he knew, then all the powers on this earth would not get him to go through with this business once again. As the Yanks said, the bandleader had had it *up to here*.

Smith made his decision. They'd get it over and done with and then they'd race like hell back to Luxembourg City and the safety of Bradley's HQ. Someone else could take over from there. He flashed a glance at his watch. It was nearly eight. It was almost time for the clandestine station to go on the air.

'We usually start off,' Habe was saying, 'with a quotation from Hitler. The intention is, Major, to show just what a liar and hypocrite the Führer is. Naturally, we want to make it clear we didn't make the quote up, but that it came straight from the, er, horse's mouth.' He beamed at Miller, pleased at his use of colloquial English.

Miller nodded. He was not too much interested in the propaganda, Smith could see that. Probably, he was concentrating mentally on his music and the commentary he would give in his halting German.

'Tonight we commence with a quote from Hitler's *Mein Kampf* to the effect that everyone is justified in rebelling; indeed, it is his duty to do so ... *Nicht nur das Recht, sondern Pflicht.*' He cited the German text as if Miller could understand, while Smith cocked his head to one side again. Yet again he thought he heard something strange outside, an unusual noise. But, strain as he might, all he heard was the howl and hiss of the raging snowstorm outside.

'Then we crack a little joke or pass on a bit of malicious gossip.' He consulted his crib. 'Tonight it is about two officers of the 532nd Engineer Battalion: a Major Krebs and a Captain Grab ... How they've brought a couple of French whores from a cathouse in Metz with them and are tucked up nice and snug for the winter while their engineers freeze their butts off. That kind of thing.' His voice tailed away and the smile vanished as Miller made it quite clear by the expression on his face that he was not really interested in this penny-ante stuff. 'Then *you're* on, Major.'

For the first time since Smith had known him, Glenn Miller came to life. He pushed his garrison cap to the back of his head and said, 'I've done a new interpretation of my "Little Brown Jug", put in a bit of Kraut oompah music, and one of the guys in the band is singing *"Ach, Du Liebe Augustin"* sort of thing.'

'Excellent, excellent,' Habe gushed. 'The young Krauts will love it. Mr Glenn Miller personally playing to them ... and in German. We'll be a great success.'

It was time now, Smith told himself, to step in. He had an unpleasant feeling that something was going to happen this stormy night. It would be better that he got out of the place sooner rather than later. 'All right, gentlemen,' he broke into the little impromptu conference as, at the generators, the technicians got on with making ready for the opening of the nightly transmission and the man in charge of the actual transmission went from mike to mike testing them. 'Let me explain my part in these proceedings. And may I make this point first. I want everything to go off without a hitch. We've got to make it snappy.'

'Rest assured,' Habe answered somewhat hotly, as if his personal honour was being attacked, 'we haven't aborted a transmission yet. Naturally, as a clandestine station we have to give the impression that we're broadcasting on the hoof, with the Gestapo hot on our trail.' He looked hard at the other man.

'Yes, yes, Captain. I understand that you always do an excellent job, and will do now. I just wanted to make the point that, this particular night with that damned snowstorm howling out there, time is not on our side. We've got to keep strictly to the timetable and, when it's all over, take a powder.'

He gave a little shiver and Habe, a perceptive man, asked, 'Something wrong, sir?'

Smith forced a little laugh. 'No. As we say in English, a ghost walked over my grave just then.' He tried to laugh again and failed. For, with the certainly of a sudden vision, he knew that there was something wrong, definitely wrong, and whatever it was, it was to be found outside.

Now the whole of the Wotan survivors were assembled to the east of the hilltop radio station. The snow was still coming down in a solid, white wall, for which they were grateful. Each of them, shrouded in snow as they crouched there in the ditch shivering, might have been the last man left alive in the whole wide world. And each was wrapped in his own cocoon of fears and apprehensions.

Von Dodenburg, squatting next to Schulze and Matz, sensed the mood of his troops. He knew it well. Even the old hares suffered from it before an attack commenced: that instant when they had to break the spell, transform themselves into killing machines and perhaps even be killed themselves. There was no decision in the world like the one he would soon have to make: to order men to stand up, attack and perhaps be killed.

Schulze broke into the heavy, brooding silence. 'I could nobble the guard at the door with one hand behind my back and my eyes closed. A proper piss-pansy, probably. But those doors, as far as I can see,' he squinted through the darkness and the flying snow, 'are going to be tough nuts. Especially if they're locked.'

'Agreed,' von Dodenburg replied.

To his left Matz whispered, 'We've got the two panzer fists, sir. Remember?'

That cheered von Dodenburg. 'Of course. Bring 'em up. We're not taking chances now. We'll blast all hell out of 'em.'

'In like Blücher!' Schulze snorted, happy that the CO, to whom he was almost slavishly devoted despite his general hatred of authority, was snapping out of his blue mood. 'They'll put the wind up the Amis' fat arses.'

Von Dodenburg agreed. 'Left, Matz ... Right flank, Schulze.' For a long moment he peered through the flying snowflakes at their worn familiar faces. Then he said with feeling in his hard voice, 'Take care, you two rogues. I'd miss you and your insubordinate thieving ways if anything...' he didn't finish his words.

'With permission, sir,' Schulze said, 'but please knock it off. You'll have me crying in my beer next, sir.' But the big NCO was obviously moved as he and Matz slipped away to carry out orders.

Von Dodenburg shook his head and then

he remembered the task in hand. As he heard the first muted strains of what the German authorities called contemptuously *nigger-Jewish monkey music*, he stood up. In that firm, confident voice that he knew young soldiers expected from their commanders on the battlefield he ordered, *'On your feet!'* They rose as one. *'Fix bayonets!'* There was that awesome final sound of the bayonet being attached to the muzzle of a weapon. He waited a fraction of a second till he was sure they were ready and then, without turning, he commanded, 'Wotan will advance ... *To the attack!'*

Inside the studio everything was proceeding as smoothly as it should. Next to Habe, Glenn Miller was tapping his foot in tune with 'Little Brown Jug', face keen, lips moving slightly, as if he were singing along with his band. Next to him Habe listened too, cue pad in his hand, ready to break in. To both sides of them the technicians and sound engineers twiddled and adjusted their dials, while less skilled men waited to carry out any adjustment. Watching anxiously, his mind on what might be happening outside, Smith flashed his anxious gaze to the dial of his wristwatch time and time again, as if he couldn't get out of this place soon enough.

The engineer in charge raised his hand,

spreading three fingers. It was the sign for three seconds to go. Miller nodded. Habe flashed a look at his cue. The transmission engineer poised himself above his dial to turn down the music, eyes watching the flickering green needle as if his life depended upon it. Up at the water cooler, the orderly hurriedly filled a paper cup with water for Habe, just in case he needed to wet his lips and throat. All seemed perfectly normal, the sort of thing that Glenn Miller must have done a thousand times or more since he had started his music career back in what now seemed another age. Ten minutes more and it would all be over and they could go back to Luxembourg City. Smith started to relax. The tension was easier. Perhaps his nerves were shot by the years he had spent in the secret war in the shadows where every man's hand had been against him. Perhaps it was time he took a rest.

The rocket from the *panzerfaust* slammed into the door with startling suddenness. It was followed an instant later by another. The door splintered. Another hammer-blow, like that of a gigantic metal fist, and one wing flew off its hinges. The studio was filled with acrid, choking smoke. Smith drew his Colt. From outside came the bass cheer of a couple of score of lusty young men charging into battle. '*Alles für Deutschland!*' They yelled the battle cry of Regiment

Wotan in bold abandon.

In the studio panic broke out. Smith heard the clatter of heavy, nailed boots on the steps leading into the studio. All around Smith, standing there pistol in his hand, waiting for them to come, the staff ran back and forth, wondering which way to escape, their eyes wide and wild with unreasoning panic. Smith didn't even seem to notice. He knew it was the end of the road. At the mike, Glenn Miller called something to him. Was it a cry for help, information, rage? No one ever knew.

Suddenly the last stanza of 'Little Brown Jug' boomed and echoed down the long corridor, 'Little brown jug I love thee!' And then the first white ghost came skidding into the entrance and Smith commenced firing, standing boldly upright, one hand behind his back as if he were on some peace-time range. The lights went out.

# Envoi

*Ende gut, alles gut*
          *German Saying*

As far as is known, Eisenhower's classified message of 22 December 1944 releasing the news that Major Glenn Miller had been reported missing since December 15, is the last recorded instance of the Supreme Commander's involvement in the Glenn Miller mystery. Privately, he did offer his condolences to Miller's family back in the States. Thereafter, silence as far as the future president of the United States was concerned.

Even in his post-war memoirs on the campaign in Europe, General Eisenhower does not mention Miller. It seems that, for the ex-Supreme Commander and the top brass who fawned on Miller during the war, the Miller business was too much of a hot potato. It was better that they forgot it and kept everything from the general public, who might ask awkward questions.

Even ex-Colonel David Niven, the likeable British Hollywood star and Miller's immediate boss, makes no reference to Miller in his post-war, light-hearted autobiography. And it must be remembered that such accounts of movie and stage stars' lives depend for their success – *and sales* – upon name dropping and interesting anecdotes of the greats the subject has encountered on his way to stardom. The Miller disappearance, supposedly on the afternoon of December 15 1944, would have made an exciting chapter. Many thousands of Miller fans would probably have bought the book just to read the Briton's account of their hero's disappearance.

Since that penultimate weekend before the end of World War Two, there have been scores of these fans and other researchers in the UK and USA – even as far afield as India – who have tried to solve the mystery of the great bandleader's disappearance. They have all failed.

One thing they have proved conclusively is this: Glenn Miller didn't take off in a Norseman aircraft from a tiny British field in the home counties that foggy December afternoon over half a century ago. No plane did. So, if Miller was on the Continent already at that time, as most of the researchers surmise, how did he get there and when? And what happened to him afterwards?

Naturally, as in all such cases there might have been a cover-up. In Miller's case there appears really to have been one. Since the institution of the US Freedom of Information Act – proposed by that ill-fated *Tricky Dicky*, President Nixon – researchers have been allowed access to Major Miller's official 201 Personal File.

At first the access was limited. Understandably so. The authorities pleaded – rightly – that they were trying to protect Major Miller's family. So, they weren't prepared to release everything. But over the years, the decades, as the family died, more and more documents were released until there was only one left. It was the key AAF AG Form 66–2. This would have contained the details of Miller's last few days, accounting for his actions and movements till the very end, as Military Law demands.

Unfortunately, Form 66–2 had been removed from the Glenn Miller file. When this was discovered nearly five decades after the event, it was clear that the only people who could have done this were its custodians, the members of the Adjutant General's Department. But what officer, especially a career one, would dare to conceal a document that might reveal the final truth of what happened to a fellow officer and one of the most important bandleaders of our age? Apart from all other considerations, the person in question could have been subjected to criminal proceedings if discovered.

For the concealment of an official document is still an offence under the terms of the US Code of Military Justice.

There is, I feel, only one explanation for regular officers risking their careers by removing this key document. They were ordered to do so by someone at the very top of the military. And that person could only have been the Supreme Commander, General Dwight D. Eisenhower himself.

But why would Ike have concerned himself with Glenn Miller, as far as the military were concerned a relatively unimportant Major? Was it something to do with that strange mission which we suppose Glenn Miller undertook to Luxembourg? We know he went there. We know that he recorded his records in London some time that winter, and reluctantly recorded a German commentary. There is even a picture extant of his doing so. Why? Indeed there are a lot of *why's* connected with Major Glenn Miller right to the very end of his career.

Indeed, what is one to make of the fact that the official press release announcing his disappearance was not published till eighteen hundred hours on Christmas Eve 1944? It seems almost that the military authorities clung to the hope that Miller would turn up in time for the great Christmas Eve broadcast link-up between his band performing at the Olympia Theatre in Paris and an audience in the States. Why should Eisenhower still hope that Miller would appear a week after he had been reported missing in that Norseman flight on the afternoon of Friday December 15 1944?

Did the man in the trenchcoat from the State Department still expect him? Or had Smith – the only name we have for that mysterious pseudo-American from Phillips Academy – pulled off a rescue attempt after all? Was he trying to prepare an understandably upset Miller for his last great stage appearance of World War Two? So many questions and pathetically few answers.

Yet today, if you drive along that hilltop road from Echternacht to Luxembourg City, the same route that von Dodenburg and his SS Assault Regiment Wotan took so long ago, you can still see the red-and-white coloured radio masts of Radio Anni. The station has long been disused. Squatters now live in the handful of nearby cottages which once housed Captain Hans Habe's strange, multi-lingual staff. But the facade of the 1920s building is still intact, save near the art deco door. There you can see the pockmarks of bullets and shell splinters like the symptoms of some loathsome skin disease disfiguring the stone surroundings. As if graven in biblical tablets, the evidence is still there. Once, long ago, violent action took place here and young men, friend and foe, died and vanished without explanation. So, the mystery continues. It is like when you throw a stone into a still pond and ripples spread outwards, on and on and on, as if they might go on for ever.